Rachel the Clever and Other Jewish Folktales

Rachel the Clever and Other Jewish Folktales

selected and retold by
Josepha Sherman

A *Sue Katz & Associates, Inc.* Book

August House Publishers, Inc.
LITTLE ROCK

Published by August House, Inc.,
P.O. Box 3223, Little Rock, Arkansas, 72203,
501-372-5450
A Sue Katz & Associates, Inc. Book

Printed in the United States of America

10 9 8 7 6 5 4 3 2 1

LIBRARY OF CONGRESS CATALOGING-IN-PUBLICATION DATA
Sherman, Josepha.
Rachel the clever
and other Jewish folktales / selected and retold by
Josepha Sherman. — 1st ed.
p.   cm.
ISBN 0-87483-306-X (hb: alk. paper) : $18.95
ISBN 0-87483-307-8 (pb.: alk. paper) : $9.95
1. Legends, Jewish—Juvenile literature. 2. Tales. 3. Jewish folk literature. I. Title.
BM530.S486 1993
398.2'089'924—dc20   92-45069
CIP

First Edition, 1993

Executive editor: Liz Parkhurst
Project editor: Kathleen Harper
Design director: Ted Parkhurst
Cover design: Harvill-Ross Studios, Inc
Cover design and text illustrations: Jeanne Seagle
Typography: Lettergraphics / Little Rock
This book is printed on archival-quality paper which meets the
guidelines for performance and durability of the Committee on
Production Guidelines for Book Longevity of the
Council on Library Resources.

AUGUST HOUSE, INC.   PUBLISHERS   LITTLE ROCK

Contents

Introduction

O nce upon a time ... "
There isn't a group of people anywhere in the world who haven't heard those magical words, or words very much like them, or who don't know that they mean a story is about to follow. The Jews are no exception.

The stories told by Jews reflect the experiences of a people who were persecuted for their religion down through the ages. Many Jews were killed for no reason other than that they were Jews. The survivors have been scattered throughout the world.

Nowadays, although there are only about 15 million Jews in the world, they can be found in practically every country from China to Mexico. Most live either in Israel or in the United States. Nearly all of the stories in this book are those told by immigrants to America, although most of the tales are much older than the United States. Some of them were first written down in the Talmud, which is a huge collection of religious thought and folklore that was put together about the second century C.E. (which stands for Christian Era, the term Jews use instead of A.D. or *anno Domini*), but many are older even than that.

When people travel for a long time, whether they're traveling because they want to travel, or because they're fleeing for their lives, they take their folktales, their familiar, magical stories, with them. But those tales tend to rub up against the tales of the people among whom they travel, losing a bit of story here, picking up a bit of story there. Jewish folktales are as full of transformed princes, magical beings, and happy endings as those of anyone else, showing how they've been changed by the countries through which their tellers traveled—but those stories also keep that certain something that makes them especially Jewish. In Jewish folktales, this special element is usually an emphasis on doing the right thing, on surviving by cleverness and kindness—and on the need for keeping a good sense of humor!

Magical Tales

The Sorcerer's Apprentice

A FOLKTALE FROM CENTRAL ASIA

Once upon a time, a poor man and his young son, Dov, went to the sultan's city to beg. There in the palace courtyard, Dov saw a sorcerer performing. And oh, what wonderful tricks that sorcerer worked! As Dov watched, he turned water to wine, wine to water. He changed a dog to a cat, a cat to a bird, a bird to a fish.

"Father," Dov cried, "please apprentice me to that sorcerer!"

"A ... a sorcerer?" asked Dov's father. "Are you sure?"

Dov was very sure. The sorcerer studied the boy with his cold, cold eyes, and nodded. "He will do. I agree to teach this boy sorcery for three years," he told Dov's father. "You may not see him for that time. But at the end of those three years, you may come for your son."

Three years came, three years went. Dov's father trudged all the long, weary way to where the sorcerer's house lay hidden in the wilderness. The sorcerer told him, "I have turned my daughter and your son into two doves. If you can pick which dove is your son, you may leave with him. Otherwise, the boy stays with me forever."

Dov's father tried. But who can tell the difference between two doves? Weeping with despair, he wandered off into the wilderness and slept. But in a dream from heaven, an old man told him, "Pick several stalks of rye. Throw the seeds on the ground, and the two doves will start to peck it up. But one dove will eat slowly. That is your son, longing for you."

Dov's father did as the dream told him. Sure enough, one dove ate the seeds slowly, and the man cried, "That one is my son!"

Instantly Dov was in his right shape again.

The sorcerer was furious. "You may have your son back," he muttered, "but first he must agree not to work any magic while I live."

Dov stared at the sorcerer. No magic—after he'd learned so much in these three years! But what could he say? He didn't want to be the sorcerer's prisoner. Dov agreed, and he and his father left.

But as they walked, Dov noticed how thin his father had become while searching for him, how old and threadbare his clothes were. "Father," he decided, "I shall help you. I'm going to turn myself into a splendid horse, and you must sell me at market for a hundred gold pieces. Only be sure not to sell my bridle, or I'll never be able to turn back into a man!"

His father nervously agreed. Dov turned himself into a splendid horse, black as night, gleaming like ebony. On his head was a bridle of fine red leather. Dov's father took the horse to market.

Ah, but who could have expected this? The sorcerer himself was in that market, disguised as a merchant, and of course he recognized Dov at once.

"How much do you want for that horse?" the sorcerer asked.

"A hundred gold pieces," Dov's father answered.

"So much? Then let us see if he's worth it!"

With that, the sorcerer leaped onto the horse's back, tearing the reins from the man's hand. "You broke your word to me!" the sorcerer shouted in Dov's ear. "Now you are mine!"

He dug his spurs into the horse's side and galloped away.

The sorcerer stabled the horse in his own stable. He gave it no food or water, nor did he remove the fine red leather bridle. But when the sorcerer was asleep in his house, his daughter, who was as kind as her father was cruel, slipped out to the stable. The first thing she did was give the poor horse food and water. The second thing she did was stare long and hard into the horse's eyes. And the third thing she did was remove that leather bridle.

Suddenly Dov was himself again. "Thank you!" he gasped.

"I knew it was you," she whispered. "Oh, but you can't stay here—my father will kill you! Hurry, go!"

"Someday I will return to you," Dov promised.

Then he turned into a dove and flew away.

The sorcerer woke, saw the dove, and recognized it. Quickly he turned himself into a hawk and flew after it.

Dov looked back and saw the hawk speeding closer and closer, faster than any dove could fly. He saw the cruel, sharp talons reaching out to crush him!

Just as the hawk was about to catch him, Dov changed from dove to ring, and dropped safely into the sea.

The hawk dropped, too, turning into a duck, hunting for the ring in the water. But a wave washed the ring safely to shore, where the sultan's daughter was walking with her ladies. She saw the ring glittering on the sand, and slipped it on her finger.

"What a lovely ring," the princess said. "I think I will keep it."

But once she was home, the princess felt the ring tighten, squeezing her finger so painfully that she tugged it off. It fell to the floor, and Dov was himself once more.

"Please don't be afraid," Dov pleaded. "I won't hurt you. And I'm every bit as human as you." Quickly he explained who he was, adding, "A cruel sorcerer is after me, and if he catches me, he'll kill me!"

"I won't let him," the princess said bravely.

Sure enough, the sorcerer arrived at the palace. He pretended to be a merchant, but once he was alone with the princess, he promised her mountains of gold for the ring.

"I don't want your mountains of gold," the princess said.

"But I must have the ring!" the sorcerer shouted. "It's very important to me!"

"I don't believe you."

At last the raging sorcerer tried to grab the ring right off her hand, but the princess threw the ring to the ground.

The ring became a pea.

The sorcerer became a hen, trying to peck up the pea.

The pea became a weasel that quickly wrung the hen's neck!

Dov turned back into his rightful shape, bowing low to the princess. "I can never thank you enough for your help."

And then he flew back to the sorcerer's daughter, whom he loved, and who loved him. They were wed. From then on, it was the young sorcerer, not the old, who performed in the sultan's city. And because he and his wife used their magic only to help people, not to hurt them, they lived happily from then on.

The Dancing Demons

A FOLKTALE FROM RUSSIA

Once, long ago and far away, there lived two brothers, Moishe and Pinkas. Now, God had willed it that both brothers were hunchbacks, but they were as different in all other ways as day is from night. Moishe was a happy, friendly fellow, while Pinkas was a greedy, grasping soul, never pleased with anything he had. Pinkas was forever trying to pick a fight with his brother, and one day he succeeded.

"You go out of your way to be mean to everyone," Moishe told him, "but I'm not going to stay here and let you make me as miserable as you!"

With that, Moishe set out for a long walk in the forest. So long a walk was it that night overtook him in the middle of a small clearing in the wilderness. Hungry and tired, Moishe longed for his nice, warm bed in his nice, warm house. But he knew he would never be able to find his way home in the darkness.

Moishe sighed. "It won't hurt me to go to bed hungry for just one night," he said. Creeping into the hollow of a tree, Moishe curled up and settled down to sleep as best he could.

It seemed to Moishe that he had barely closed his eyes before all at once the silence of the night was broken by a terrific clang, clang, clang, and bang, bang, bang! He opened his eyes—and gasped in amazement. That once empty clearing was now full of the most incredible creatures! Some were tall, some were small, some skinny, some fat—but all had long, sharp claws, huge, glowing eyes, and great, curling horns.

"Demons!" Moishe gasped.

Beating on drums, whirling and yelling at the top of their screechy voices, they had come there in the middle of the night to dance.

One small demon stopped in the middle of a spin, sniffing and sniffing. "There!" he cried, pointing at Moishe. "A human!"

Before Moishe could run, the demons dragged him from his hiding place. "Come, human, dance with us," they insisted.

What could he do? The demons were all about him. So Moishe danced. He danced with all his might, singing as best he could, and the demons all laughed with wonder.

"Why, you are a fine dancer," they cried, "the finest dancer we have ever seen. You must stay with us forever!"

"Oh, no!" Moishe gasped. All the demons glared, so he added quickly, "I can't stay with you just yet. You see, I … I have business back at home that I must look after."

That made sense to the demons. "But if you leave us," asked the small demon, "how do we know you will ever come back?"

"I will," Moishe promised.

"Yes, you will," the demons agreed, "and to make sure you do, you're going to leave us a pledge."

What could Moishe leave as a pledge? He had nothing on him but his shirt, trousers, and shoes, which the demons refused. "But what else can I give you?" cried Moishe. "I have nothing left but ... but my hump!"

"Why, that's a *fine* pledge!" cried the demons.

With that, they took the hump from his back, as easily and painlessly as could be, and Moishe hurried home straight-backed and amazed. By the time he reached his village, he was no longer running but walking, shoulders back, head up.

Pinkas stared at his brother. "What happened to you?" he asked. "Where is your hump?"

Moishe told him all that had happened.

"But everyone knows demons have hoards of gold!" Pinkas said. "You fool! If you had only been a little cleverer, you could have taken their gold away with you."

Moishe smiled. "I'm quite happy with things as they are, brother."

That wasn't good enough for Pinkas. He brooded and brooded over what had happened to his brother, and finally decided, "I will win that gold for myself."

So he set off for the clearing in the forest, curled up in the hollow of the tree, and fell asleep. Sure enough, that night there came the same terrific clang, clang, clang, and bang, bang, bang! Pinkas opened his eyes to see the demons whirling about, beating their drums and yelling at the top of their screechy voices.

"Wait, wait!" cried the small demon. "A human is watching us!"

The demons dragged Pinkas from his hiding place. "Come, human, you will dance with us," they insisted.

Pinkas danced. He was a terrible dancer, and a worse singer, but his horrible screaming sounded simply wonderful to the demons. Alas for Pinkas, demons can't tell one human being from another.

"You have returned!" they cried in glee. "Our marvelous singer and dancer has returned. You honest man, you really *have* returned to us!"

"Uh ... yes," Pinkas said, looking about for their gold. "Of course I have."

"We shall return your pledge to you," the demons said, "and you shall never, ever leave us."

Before Pinkas could say a thing, they brought his brother's hump to him and slapped it on top of his own hump. And what happened to him after that? Did he go on dancing with the demons for all time? No one can say. But Moishe never saw his greedy, grasping brother again.

Cinderella

A FOLKTALE FROM POLAND

Once, in the long ago days, there lived a man who had three daughters. But one day he began to wonder if those daughters really loved him, so he called them to him one by one and asked, "How much do you love me?"

The eldest daughter never stopped to think. "I love you as much as gold," she answered.

"Very good!" her father said.

The second daughter never stopped to think, either. "I love you as much as silver," she answered.

"Not quite as good," said her father, "but good enough."

But when he asked his youngest daughter, Sonye, "How much do you love me?" she answered, "Why, I love you as much as meat loves salt."

As much as meat loves salt? What manner of foolish answer was this? "You don't love me at all!" shouted the man, and he threw his youngest daughter out of his house.

Weeping, Sonye wandered on. Night came, and day, and night again, and she still wandered. Where could she go? Where could she find shelter?

Suddenly an old man appeared in front of her. Though Sonye didn't know it, this was none other than the Prophet Elijah, who sometimes, stories say, appears to help those in trouble.

"Where are you going, my child?" he asked.

His voice was so kind that Sonye found herself telling him her whole story.

"Don't be afraid," the old man said gently. "All will still end well, if you do as I tell you. Take this stick."

It looked like nothing more than a plain twig, but Sonye thanked him and tucked it into the sash of her dress.

"Stay on this path," continued the old man, "till you come to a house where you can hear someone saying the proper blessing over food. Be sure to add 'Amen.' You will be invited inside, but don't enter till the rabbi himself asks you to enter. Once you're inside, hide the stick in the attic. Whenever you need anything, all you have to do is tell the stick, 'Stick, open!'"

With that, the old man disappeared. Sonye went on her way until she came to a house that was cheerful with light. She heard someone saying the blessing over food, and added, in the proper place, "Amen."

The people inside hurried outside. The rabbi whose house it was asked Sonye to enter, and she thanked him and did. She looked so dirty and ragged from her wanderings that everyone thought she was only a poor little beggar girl. They gave her some food and a place to sleep beside the stove.

That night, Sonye crept upstairs as the old man had told her to do, and hid the magic stick in the attic.

The next day, the rabbi and his family dressed in their best clothes and left for a wedding. Poor, lonely Sonye. How she wanted to go with them! But how could she go to a wedding in her dirty old clothes?

Suddenly Sonye remembered the magic stick. She climbed up to the attic, picked up the stick, and told it, "Stick, open!"

The stick opened wide, and inside was a cake of soap and a basin of water. Once Sonye had washed off all the dirt from her travels, she said again, "Stick, open!"

The stick opened wide, and inside were dainty golden shoes and a wonderful gown covered with golden embroidery. Dressed in this beautiful clothing, Sonye went to the wedding. There she met Mendl, the rabbi's son, tall and handsome as any prince. Mendl took one look at this lovely stranger and fell madly in love. (Never did he recognize the dirty little beggar girl who had crouched beside the stove.) He begged her to tell him who she was, but Sonye would not answer.

Ah, but Mendl was a clever young man. He spread pitch on the doorstep. When it was time for the wedding guests to leave, the mysterious stranger tried to hurry away, but she stepped right in the pitch, and one golden shoe stuck to it. She ran away without it. Mendl lost the beautiful stranger, but he picked up her shoe.

By the time the rabbi, his wife, and Mendl returned home, Sonye had already hidden her fine clothes. Smeared with dirt, dressed in her rags, she crouched by the side of the stove. No one dreamed she had ever moved from it.

Mendl searched high and he searched low for the owner of the golden shoe, but not one maiden would it fit. At last, after days of hopeless hunting, he returned home, sad and weary.

"Let me try on the shoe," Sonye said.

"What, a poor little beggar girl?" Mendl asked with a laugh.

She snatched the shoe from his hand—and of course that shoe fit her perfectly.

The rabbi and his wife cried out in horror. What, their son marry a dirty little beggar girl? That must never be!

But the next morning, the rabbi said to his wife, "I had a most disturbing dream. In it, a strange old man appeared and warned me not to stop the wedding."

"Why, I had exactly the same dream!" his wife cried. "What can this mean?"

Worried, they went out for a walk, to think about what they should do. Mendl was left alone with Sonye.

"Come with me," Sonye said. "See who I really am."

She led him up to the attic and picked up the magic stick. "Stick, open!"

The stick opened wide, and inside it were wonderful clothes, heavy with silver embroidery.

"See?" Sonye said. "There are some for you, some for me."

Dressed as finely as a prince and princess, they went for a walk, arm in arm, talking happily together.

"Will you forgive me for not recognizing you?" Mendl asked.

"I will. But you must remember to see the girl, not the rich clothes!" Sonye scolded.

"I will," Mendl promised.

Meanwhile, the rabbi and his wife saw the beautiful couple from a distance. Surely this was still part of their dream, their handsome son walking arm in arm with a lovely stranger?

"It *can't* be Mendl!" the rabbi gasped. "He has no clothes so fine."

"Besides," the rabbi's wife added, "he's still at home."

"Come, let's hurry back and see."

But by the time the rabbi and his wife reached their house, Sonye and Mendl had already changed into their old clothes.

"Father, Mother," Mendl said firmly, "I love this beggar girl. I'm going to marry her, and that's that."

The rabbi and his wife sighed. "Then marry her," they said reluctantly, "you shall."

They sent out wedding invitations far and wide. One of those who accepted the invitation was Sonye's father. When she learned he was coming to her wedding, she rushed to the kitchen. There she told the cooks who were preparing the wedding feast, "Be sure you cook one meal with no salt in it at all."

The wedding day came. "Stick, open!" Sonye said, and inside were clothes even more wonderful than before, heavy with gold and silver embroidery. Mendl and Sonye were once more as splendid as a prince and his princess. The rabbi and his wife were amazed to realize that the beggar girl and the beautiful girl were one and the same.

"We should have looked at the girl, not the clothing," they told each other.

After the wedding ceremony, everybody feasted.

Only one man did not feast, and that was Sonye's father. No, he only sat staring sadly at his food.

The bride came up to him, her veil hiding her face. "You don't seem to be enjoying your meal," she said.

"Alas, how can I? This food has no salt in it at all."

"Now you understand!" Sonye cried, and pushed back her veil. "Father, dear Father, do you remember when you asked me how much I loved you? Do you remember what I said?"

Her father nearly wept for joy. "You told me you loved me as much as meat loves salt! Oh Sonye, my dear, dear daughter, can you ever forgive me for what I've done?"

Sonye smiled. "If I hadn't left home," she said, looking at Mendl, "I never would have met my husband."

She had a fresh meal brought to her father. This one was properly salted!

And everyone lived joyfully from that day on.

The Sultan's Horns

A FOLKTALE FROM MOROCCO

Once upon a time, there was a sultan who had a shameful secret. Growing from the top of his head he had two little horns, just like the horns of a goat.

"None of my people must know of this," he told himself. "They would laugh at me, and the rulers of other lands would laugh at me as well!"

But hair grows as it will, and even a sultan has need of a barber. Each time the sultan had his hair cut, he called for a different barber, and as soon as the man said something about the sultan's horns, why, the sultan had him thrown into prison.

At last there were no barbers left in the royal city, none save one poor man named Selim.

When the sultan's order came to Selim, telling him he must cut the sultan's hair, he trembled. What had happened to all those other barbers? But Selim had no choice. The soldiers of the sultan took him straight to the palace.

Selim cut the sultan's hair. Sure enough, he saw the sultan's horns, but he bit his lip to keep from saying anything about them.

"Do you see anything strange about me?" the sultan asked.

Selim shook his head.

"Nothing strange at all?"

Selim shook his head again.

"Come now, you have seen my horns. I swear you to silence, barber: you must never tell anyone what you have seen here, on pain of death!"

Selim swore. The sultan let him go, and Selim hurried home. When his wife asked him what the sultan was like, he only shook his head and said nothing, but the secret of those horns began to haunt him. He didn't dare speak to anyone in case the truth should pop out. He didn't dare sleep, in case he told the truth in his dreams.

Every day the weight of the secret pressed down on poor Selim more heavily. At last, just when he thought he must burst, he had a wonderful idea. Selim hurried to a cave near the city. No one was around. He shouted into the cave, "The sultan has goat horns!"

Oh, how much better he felt! Selim went happily home.

Reeds grew near the cave. A shepherd boy cut them to make himself a flute. He took his sheep to town, playing happily on his flute as he did. But the only song that flute would play was "The sultan has goat horns!"

The news spread quickly. Soon all the city had heard it. The furious sultan had Selim dragged before him.

"I warned you to say nothing of this to anyone!" he shouted at the trembling barber. "I warned you on pain of death."

"But ... but I didn't tell anyone!" Selim protested. "Not anyone alive!"

Hastily, he told the sultan what he had done. The sultan sighed.

"Go home, Selim," he said. "You are free. And guards, release all the captive barbers, too."

The truth will come out, no matter how hard men try to stop it.

The Son Who Was a Snake

A FOLKTALE FROM MIDDLE EUROPE

Once upon a time there lived a husband and wife who had everything anyone could want save one thing only: a child. So one day they went to a wise old rabbi and asked for his help.

The rabbi went to the synagogue and prayed for wisdom, and at last he returned to the husband and wife.

"With God's help," he told them, "you will have a son, but first you must hold a feast to celebrate Rosh Hodesh, the coming of the new month. Invite one and all, rich and poor. If a stranger appears, you must give him the place of honor at the head of the table. Do this, and all will be well."

"We will!" the happy couple promised.

They went home and prepared a wonderful Rosh Hodesh feast of fine food and drink, and invited everyone in the town to join them. But in the middle of their happy feasting, a stranger appeared. Oh, he was a ragged, dirty old man!

The husband and wife looked at each other in dismay. What, this dirty old beggar sit in the place of honor? Maybe if they ignored him, he would go away.

But the old beggar man didn't go away. He insisted on sitting in the place of honor.

"No, no, you don't understand," the husband said, taking him gently by the arm. "This table is already full." He led the beggar to a small table where poorer folk were sitting. "Here is a fine seat for you, and plenty of good food to eat."

But the old beggar man refused to sit down. "I must speak to you and your wife," he said, and marched right back up to the head of the main table. "Hear me," he told the husband and wife, "and hear me well. You have forgotten the rabbi's advice. You refused to give a stranger the place of honor, and so all will *not* be well. You shall have your son, yes—but he shall be not a boy, but a snake!"

With that, the old man disappeared.

Oh, the husband and wife sorrowed long and hard after that. But as time passed, they began to take the old man's strange words less seriously.

"He must have been a madman, poor thing. Who listens to what a madman says?"

But then, nine months later, the old man's words came true. The wife gave birth not to a boy, but to a snake, a strange, golden snake like none ever seen before. The husband and wife wept for a time over this sadness.

"But ... he *is* our son," the husband said at last.

His wife agreed, "Snake though he may be, he is our son."

And as the days passed and the snake grew, he showed a good son's wit and kindness. Slowly the husband and wife came to love him. At last they all but forgot that he was a snake, not a boy, and raised him like any other child, educating him in all the proper ways.

So the years passed.

One day the snake came to his parents and said, "Father, Mother, I am now old enough to wed. Please, find me a bride. I will return home in a month for the wedding."

With that, he vanished into the forest.

"What can we do?" wailed the wife. "Who will want to marry a snake? How can our poor son ever be happy?"

Off the husband and wife went to the wise old rabbi.

"You didn't listen to me once," he said to them, "yet you want me to help you again."

"Oh, please!" the wife cried. "It's not for us, but for our son. What woman will wed him? What bride won't run from him in fright?"

The rabbi went to the synagogue and prayed. At last he returned, and told them, "God has a solution to every problem. Go find the poorest man in town and share the Sabbath with him. There you will find a bride for your son."

Off the couple went to the hovel of the poorest man in town. To their bewilderment, though, on Friday night the poor man set out two dishes for his guests, one for his wife, one for himself—and five extra dishes. Without a word of explanation, he took those five dishes into another room. He did the same thing for the next Sabbath meal, on Saturday.

The husband and wife could no longer keep from asking, "Why do you keep bringing those five plates of food into another room?"

The poor man sighed. "I have five daughters. But they are ashamed to be seen by guests in their rags, so they're hiding in that room."

"We will buy them fine clothes," the husband and wife told him. "Then let us meet them."

Soon, out came the five daughters in their fine new clothes. Each in turn was asked the same question: "Would you marry our snake-son?"

One by one the daughters refused. Only the youngest hesitated.

"If I leave," she said, "there will be one less mouth for my father to feed. Yes, I will marry your son."

The husband and wife took the girl home with them, but they were afraid to tell her anything about their son, and wouldn't let her see him.

The wedding day came at last. As the bride was dressing for her marriage, a large golden snake slithered in through the window.

"Don't be afraid," he whispered.

"I ... I'm not," she said.

All at once, the snake stood up on his tail, wiggling and wriggling. His skin split open, and a handsome young man stepped out.

"Who are you?" the bride gasped.

"Your husband, if you will wed me. You see, since my parents refused charity to an old man, I was born in the shape of a snake. But now the magic has all but ended. I will be a man forever if you will only keep my secret a little longer. Will you stand with a snake under the wedding canopy?"

"I ... I will."

The young man stepped back into the snakeskin. It closed about him, and he slithered from the room.

At the wedding, all the guests whispered in horror. What, a woman marry a snake? Only the bride herself was calm, even though a great golden snake was beside her under the wedding canopy.

But just as the rabbi was pronouncing them wed, the snake vanished, just like that, and in its place stood the handsome young man.

"You kept my secret," he told his bride, "and now I shall be your loving husband forever."

So it was that they all lived happily to the end of their days.

The Demon's Midwife

A FOLKTALE FROM MOROCCO

Once, long ago, Aviva the midwife was hurrying home after having helped yet another baby be born. But the night was very dark, and a gust of wind blew out Aviva's candle.

"Oh no! Now I can't see where I'm going."

Suddenly a big white cat stepped out of the darkness and rubbed itself against the midwife's legs, purring. Aviva started to pet it, but the cat stalked away, looking back over its shoulder.

"You ... you want me to follow you? Very well. I don't want to stay out here all night."

Sure enough, the white cat led Aviva right to her own front door. She told the cat, "God grant that as you helped me, I can someday help you."

A year passed.

One night, as Aviva sat at home, peacefully sewing, someone pounded on her door.

"No need to break it down," she called. "I'm coming."
There stood a tall, dark-eyed stranger wrapped in a
black cloak. "Please, come with me," he pleaded. "My wife
is about to give birth to her first child, and she needs a
midwife's help."

Well, Aviva didn't like the looks of that mysterious
stranger, but how could she refuse a woman who needed
her help? So off she and the stranger went into the night.

Whether they went a long way or a short way, Aviva
couldn't tell in all that darkness. Only by clinging to the
stranger's cloak could she keep going.

Then all at once the darkness was brightened by
hundreds of candles, and the midwife found herself enter-
ing a magnificent mansion. But she didn't have time to do
more than glance here and there at all the lovely things.
Before Aviva could even catch her breath, she was led into
a bedroom. There lay a young woman who was about to
give birth. The midwife set about her work, and soon was
welcoming a healthy baby boy into the world.

But as Aviva placed the baby at his mother's breast, the
young woman whispered to her, "Do you recognize me?
No? I am a demon woman, and all these people are demons,
too. But don't be afraid! I was also the white cat who guided
you home a year ago. Now you have helped me, so I'll help
you. When my relatives ask you to share their feast, refuse.
When they offer to reward you, take nothing but the
smallest rug that lies by the door."

Sure enough, the demons asked Aviva to join their
feast. She politely told them she was fasting. Next, they
showed her wonderful gold and silver treasures, and told

her to choose a reward. Aviva asked only for the smallest rug that lay by the door.

"My wife must have warned you," the tall, dark-eyed stranger said. "Had you eaten with us, you would have been our guest forever. Had you chosen any of those treasures, you would have been our prisoner forever. But the rug cannot harm you. Come, I shall take you home."

So he did. Aviva spread out the small rug by her bedside.

"It's a pretty thing," she said, "even if it isn't a wonderful treasure."

But when she awoke in the morning, Aviva found that the rug was covered with gold coins, and each time a coin was removed, another took its place.

"The demon woman gave me a wonderful treasure after all!"

Aviva was not a greedy woman. She shared that gold with anyone who needed help, and so she lived happily all her life.

The Tricky Sheep

A FOLKTALE FROM POLAND

Once, long ago and far away, Ruben the farmer was driving his horse and wagon home from market at the end of the day. The empty wagon rattled and bounced along the road, when all of a sudden Ruben said, "Whoa!"

A sheep lay at the side of the road. It was a nice, fat, woolly sheep, and it didn't seem to be hurt or ill. The sheep also didn't have any mark of ownership on it.

Ruben got down from his wagon. "What luck!" he said. "I don't know where you came from, sheep, but you're mine now."

He got some rope from the wagon and tied up the sheep, then hoisted it onto the wagon.

"Gee-up," Ruben told his horse. "Let's go home."

When he shook the reins, his horse leaned into its harness as though it could hardly pull the wagon.

"Come on!" Ruben said. "One sheep can't weigh all that much."

The horse strained and struggled as though the weight it was pulling were growing heavier and heavier. Ruben glanced back, but saw only that one sheep sitting in his wagon.

"No sheep can weigh that much!" he repeated.

But the night was coming on, and the wagon seemed to be getting heavier and heavier still. Ruben's heart pounded with growing fear. Would they never get home? Would they struggle on this road for ever and ever?

Then all at once, the horse bounded forward and broke into a gallop. The wagon bounced and rattled behind it.

"What ... what's going on?"

Ruben glanced over his shoulder. The sheep was no longer in the wagon—it was standing on its hind legs in middle of the road, laughing!

All at once, it wasn't a sheep at all, but a funny little demon.

"That was a wonderful trick I played on you," it called, "a wonderful trick, indeed! Good day to you, human."

And it vanished into the night.

Clever Folks

Rachel the Clever

A FOLKTALE FROM POLAND

Once, long ago, there lived a king who was very proud of his clever wits. So proud of them was he that he vowed to marry only a woman who was as clever as he.

Now, one day the king stopped at an inn. There he heard the innkeeper boasting about his daughter, Rachel, who was so clever she could solve any riddle. The king frowned.

"I don't like liars," he told the innkeeper. "I will ask you three riddles. If your daughter can solve them, you will be rewarded, but if she fails, you shall lose your inn. First, what is the fastest thing? Second, what is the richest thing? Third, what is the dearest thing?"

Sadly, the innkeeper went home to his daughter, Rachel, and told her what the king had said. Rachel smiled. "You won't lose the inn, Father. Go to the king and tell him that Thought is the fastest thing, life-giving Earth is the richest thing, and Love is the dearest thing."

When the king heard these answers, he frowned again. He had vowed to wed only a woman as clever as he. Could that woman be Rachel, a common innkeeper's daughter? "If Rachel is as clever as she seems," he told the innkeeper, "I wish to meet her. She must come to my palace in three days—but she must come neither walking nor riding, neither dressed nor undressed, and bringing a gift that is not a gift."

Sadly the innkeeper went home, sure that Rachel could never solve this puzzle. But Rachel thought for only a few moments, and then she smiled. "Don't worry, father. I know what to do. Please buy me a goat, a fishnet, and ... hmm ... two doves."

Bewildered, the innkeeper did as he was asked. Rachel wrapped herself in the fishnet and sat on the goat so that one leg dragged on the ground. Clutching the doves, she set off for the royal palace.

"I'm Rachel, the innkeeper's daughter," she told the king with a grin. "I've come to you neither riding nor walking, as you see. With this fishnet wrapped around me, I'm neither dressed nor undressed."

The king felt himself starting to smile. "And the gift that is not a gift?"

"Here!"

Rachel released the two doves. Before the king could catch them, they fluttered wildly out the window. The king burst into laughter.

"That was most certainly a gift that was not a gift!" he said.

Now, Rachel was as pretty and kind as she was clever, and the king (when he forgot about being proud) was equally handsome and just as kind. They looked at each other once, and liked what they saw. They looked at each other twice, and forgot he was a king and she was only an innkeeper's daughter. They looked at each other three times, and the king said, "I wanted to marry a clever woman. You are surely she. Rachel, will you marry me?" Rachel happily agreed.

Ah, but all at once the king remembered to be proud. "But you must never disagree with any of the judgments I make at court," he warned.

Rachel sighed. "Very well."

So the king and the innkeeper's daughter were married, and lived so happily that for a long time the king forgot about his pride. But one day Rachel saw a peasant at court with a sad, sad face.

"I own a mare that gave birth under my neighbor's wagon," he told her. "The king has ruled that the foal belongs to my neighbor."

"Why, that's not right!" cried Rachel. "Go stand under the king's window with a fishing rod and pretend you're catching fish."

The peasant obeyed. When the king asked him how he could catch fish on a marble floor, the peasant answered, as Rachel had told him, "If a wagon can give birth to a foal, then I can catch fish on a marble floor."

When the king heard this answer, he knew that only Rachel could have given it. His pride overpowered his love.

"Since you have broken our agreement," he told Rachel, "you must leave the palace." Even as he said these harsh words, the king felt his heart break. But his pride was still stronger than his love. "You must leave," he repeated, "but you may take your dearest possession with you." Rachel didn't weep or wail. Instead, she slipped a sleeping potion into the king's cup. As soon as he was sleeping soundly that evening, Rachel wrapped him in a blanket, hoisted him up onto her back, and carried him out into the night. The guards, remembering what the king had said and thinking that Rachel was carrying a golden treasure, never stopped her.

The king woke to the sound of birds, and found himself lying under a tree in the middle of a grassy field. Rachel was beside him. "What ... why ... ?" the king stammered. "What am I doing here?"

Rachel smiled gently. "I was following your order," she said. "You told me I could take my dearest possession with me. And that, my love, is you."

The king looked into Rachel's warm eyes. And as he looked, he forgot all about his pride, this time forever. "Will you forgive me?" he asked.

"Of course. And will you listen to me before you make your judgments?"

"Of course. Come, my dearest possession," said the king. "Let us go home."

Choosing Lots

A FOLKTALE FROM SPAIN

Long ago, during the Middle Ages, the king and queen of Spain decided that all who were not Catholic like themselves must either convert or be put to death. This terrible time was called the Spanish Inquisition, and many Jews and others suffered for their faith.

In the city of Seville, a rumor started that a Christian boy had been murdered by the Jewish community. This wasn't true, but the Grand Inquisitor ordered the city's rabbi to stand trial for all the Jews of Seville. The Grand Inquisitor was a cruel man who hated the Jews, and wanted to have them all killed. But the rabbi quickly proved that there wasn't any real evidence against them.

The Grand Inquisitor wasn't about to give up so easily.

"We shall leave the matter to heaven," he said to the rabbi. "I am going to place two pieces of paper in a box. On one paper will be the word 'guilty,' and on the other, the word 'innocent.' You must reach into the box and pick one piece of paper. If you draw the guilty lot, you shall be put to death. But if you draw the innocent lot, I shall let you go free."

"Fair enough," the rabbi said.

He knew, however, that the Grand Inquisitor would never play fairly. Sure enough, the Inquisitor wrote "guilty" on *both* pieces of paper.

The rabbi was ready for such a trick. When the time came for him to pick a lot, he put his hand into the box, pulled out a piece of paper—and popped it into his mouth! Before anyone could stop him, he swallowed that lot.

"What nonsense is this?" the Grand Inquisitor shouted.

"No nonsense at all," the rabbi said. "The only piece of paper remaining in the box is one marked 'guilty.' You can see it for yourself."

And of course, "guilty" is what was on that lot.

"Then," the rabbi added, smiling, "by the rules you made, the piece of paper I ate must have been marked 'innocent.' And so I, and my people, are free. Good day to you, Grand Inquisitor."

What could the Grand Inquisitor do? If he accused the rabbi of lying, then he would have to admit he'd cheated. Furious, he did the only thing he could: he stood aside and let the rabbi go free.

The Slave Who Was a Detective

A FOLKTALE FROM THE TALMUD

Over two thousand years ago, the Greeks ruled over the land we now call Israel. One day a Greek gentleman who lived in Athens decided he would travel to Israel to see what wisdom he could learn there. He lived in Israel for three years, but in all that time he didn't learn a thing.

"It's not right that a gentleman like me should have to do everything for himself," he decided. "That's why I haven't had time to learn wisdom. I need a servant."

In those days, slavery was still allowed, and so the Greek bought himself a Jewish slave named Avi who had fallen on hard times. Only after the sale was complete, though, did the Greek realize his new slave was blind in one eye.

"I can see more with one eye than you can see with two," Avi promised.

What could the Greek do? He'd already spent his money, so he started out for home through the desert with his one-eyed slave. In those days, traveling alone was a dangerous thing to do because the desert was full of robbers, so Avi cried, "Let's hurry and join the caravan that's ahead of us."

The Greek stared up the road. "I don't see any caravan. Where is it?"

Avi studied the ground. "Oh, about ... four leagues ahead of us. What's more, the lead camel is female. And she's carrying twins."

"You can't possibly know that!"

"But I do," Avi said. "What's more, that lead camel is also carrying leather bottles, one of which holds wine. The other holds vinegar. Ha, and she's blind in one eye."

"How could you know all that?" cried the Greek. "You ... you one-eyed slave, you're lying!"

Avi shrugged. "I can see well enough to see that only one side of the road has been grazed: the side the camel can see."

"And how can you know she's pregnant? And with twins!"

"See there, where she lay down to rest? There's a double depression in the sand, just the sort that a camel pregnant with two babies would leave."

The Greek scratched his head. "But ... but how do you know one bottle holds wine and the other, vinegar?"

"Oh, that's easy. Leather bottles do leak, you know. Wine soaks right into the ground, but vinegar leaves bubbles."

"All right, all right, I agree," said the Greek. "But how could you possibly know that the caravan is four leagues ahead of us?"

Avi smiled. "That's my secret."

"No, no, no!" the Greek shouted in frustration. "I have to know!"

"Free me," Avi said quietly, "and I will tell you."

"No! I paid good money for you."

"Then I'm afraid I can't tell you any more."

"But you ... I ... all right! You are free. Now, how did you know that the caravan is four leagues ahead of us?"

"Why, it was easy. I can still just make out the prints of the camels' feet. A camel's footprints become unreadable right after four leagues. Now come, if we hurry, we can catch up with the caravan."

So they hurried along. But Avi the ex-slave smiled all the way.

The Silent Duel

A FOLKTALE FROM EASTERN EUROPE

Once upon a time there lived a cruel, cold-hearted king who thought he was the cleverest man who ever ruled. One day, he challenged the Jews who lived in his royal city to a silent duel. Any Jew who dared accept the challenge and lost would be given a hundred lashes. But if no one accepted that challenge, all the Jews would be put to death.

What a terrible choice! Who would be brave enough to risk a hundred lashes?

A simple cobbler stepped forward.

"I may not be a clever man like the king," he said, "but the worst that can happen is that the king will have me put to death. All the rest of you will be spared."

The king stared down his royal nose at this humble opponent. How dare the Jews send a mere cobbler to duel with him! He would end this right away, and have them all put to death.

So the king began the silent duel by raising his forefinger.

The cobbler pointed straight down.

The king's eyes widened in surprise. He thrust two fingers at the Jew.

The cobbler thrust one finger at the king.

The king thrust out his whole hand at the Jew.

The cobbler held up his fist.

Frowning, the king held up a bottle of red wine.

Shrugging, the cobbler took a piece of white cheese out of his pocket.

"Enough!" the king cried. "You have won—name your reward."

"For me, Your Majesty, nothing. I only want you to promise not to bother the Jews again."

"Agreed," the king muttered.

Once the cobbler was gone, the king's puzzled servants asked what the silent duel had meant.

"When I pointed up," the king told them, "I was saying that the Jews were as many as the stars. The cobbler pointed down, answering that they were as the grains of sand.

"When I pointed with two fingers, I was saying there are two gods, one of good, one of evil. When he pointed with only one finger, he was saying there is only one God.

"My third gesture, with my whole hand, meant that the Jews are scattered all over the world. His fist said that the Jews are still united.

"My last gesture, holding up the wine, said his sins were red as wine. He replied that no, they were white as cheese."

Meanwhile, though, the cobbler was telling a very different story to the Jews.

"Well, first he pointed up to tell me he wanted to hang me. So I pointed down, telling him to go to the devil!

"Then he tried to poke out my eyes with his two fingers, so I pointed back, telling him it would be an eye for an eye!

"That got him really mad. He tried to slap me with his whole hand, so I warned him with my fist not to try it!

"Now the king was scared of me. He offered me a drink of wine. What could I do but be polite and offer him some cheese? And that's when he knew I had won." The cobbler shrugged. "It was easy!"

One Shot Too Many

A FOLKTALE FROM MIDDLE EUROPE

One night Moishe, a Jewish carpenter, was hurrying home from a long day's work, his wages in his pocket. But to get home, he had to pass through a forest. All at once a robber jumped out from behind a tree, pointing a gun at Moishe.

"Give me your money!" the robber ordered.

What could poor Moishe do? Only a fool argues with a man with a gun. So Moishe handed over his money, but as he did, he said, "My wife isn't going to believe I was robbed. It would be really kind of you if you would help me out just a bit."

"What do you mean?"

"Well … you could shoot a bullet through my hat so it looks as though we fought."

The robber thought that was a funny idea. He tossed Moishe's hat into the air and shot a bullet right through the brim.

"How's that?" he asked.

"Well ... you could shoot a bullet through the corner of my coat, too. Then it would really look like we had a fight."

The robber shrugged. As Moishe held out the corner of his coat, the robber shot a bullet through it, too.

"That's better," Moishe said. "But let's make it look *really* convincing. Shoot one more bullet through the other corner of my coat."

"I can't!" the robber snarled. "I'm out of bullets."

"Oh, you are, are you?" Moishe cried.

He flattened the robber with one good punch, took back his money, and went on his way, whistling.

The Questions of the King

A FOLKTALE FROM YEMEN

Once upon a time, the Sultan of the city of San'a decided that only those who followed the religion of Islam would be allowed to live in his city. That meant that all the Jews would be thrown out.

"But Your Majesty," his advisors argued, "that will make you look totally merciless."

So the sultan announced a test. If any Jew could answer his three questions, all the Jews in San'a would be allowed to stay.

Who would this be? Who was bold enough to come before the sultan? Who was wise enough to answer him? No one except a young boy named Salim. Trusting in God to see him through, he said, "Ask your questions, O mighty sultan."

At first the sultan was angry that the Jews should dare to send a mere child to answer him. But then he grew puzzled. Could it be that this young boy really was wise?

Hastily, the sultan asked his first question.

"How many stars are there in the sky?"

Salim never hesitated. "Three million, five hundred and one."

"How do you know that's the right answer?" the sultan asked.

"How do you know that it's not?" Salim replied. "If you don't believe me, you'll just have to count them all yourself."

"Very well, very well," the sultan muttered. "You win the first question. But you won't find the second question so easy!"

He led the boy out into the royal gardens. Dipping his hand into a pool, the sultan asked, "How much water is there in my gardens?"

"First, tell me how many drops of water are on your hand," Salim replied.

"That's impossible to say!"

"No more so than your question, O sultan."

"Very well," the sultan muttered. "You win the second question. But you won't find the third question so easy!"

He showed Salim three apples set on a table and asked, "How many apples are there?"

Salim hesitated. This was surely a trick. After all, the sultan had not asked how many apples were on the table. The boy shook his head and answered simply, "One."

"One! How can there be only one?"

"The 'one' means the One God. If I added two or three, that would be suggesting there are more gods. That would be against both my religion and yours, the Jewish faith and the Moslem."

The sultan drew back in surprise. What could he possibly answer to that?

"You are a wise young man," he said at last, "and you have answered my three questions well. Your people were right to send you, and the Jews of San'a may go on living in my city in peace."

The Hidden Gold

A FOLKTALE FROM THE TALMUD

Once, in the long ago days when King Saul ruled the land of Israel, a widow received a message from her sister, who lived in a foreign city. That sister was ill, and needed to see her right away.

The widow hastily packed some clothing. But she had a good many gold coins, too many to take with her. How could she safely hide them in such a short time? Quickly she emptied out some jars of honey, dropped the coins into the jars, then topped them off again with honey. Away she went to her sister, leaving the honey jars with a neighbor.

Alas, soon after, the neighbor needed some honey.

"I'll just take a little from the widow's jars," he decided.

But as soon as he scooped the honey off the top of one jar, he found the gold coins. Greed was stronger than honesty. He stole all the coins, and refilled the jars with honey.

The widow's sister recovered quickly. Soon the widow was able to go home.

Aie, but when she looked for her coins, she found only honey! The widow hurried to court, but the judges sent her away.

"We have no proof," they told her, "that the jars ever had any coins hidden in them."

The widow sadly started back for home. On her way, she passed a young shepherd boy. His name was David, and he would one day be king of Israel, but no one knew that yet. Seeing how sad she looked, he asked, "What's wrong?"

The widow sighed. "I had hidden my coins in honey jars. While I was away, my neighbor stole the coins and left only the honey. But no one will believe me!"

"I believe you," David said, "and if King Saul will allow it, I think I can help you."

The widow hurried to the king. King Saul was curious. "Let this shepherd boy do his best to solve the case!" he said.

The widow and her neighbor went to court. David had all the honey jars brought before them.

"Are these the right honey jars?" he asked. "Yes? Fine."

He began to break the jars, one after another, until at last he cried out in triumph.

"Look! Honey is sticky, as everyone knows. And see what's stuck to the inside of this jar!"

Two gold coins, overlooked by the neighbor, were clinging to the side of the jar.

"My coins!" cried the widow.

The neighbor hung his head in shame. "Your coins," he agreed.

He returned all the stolen gold to the widow. The king and all his court were amazed at the wisdom of that simple shepherd boy.

Doing Unto Others

A FOLKTALE FROM THE TALMUD

Once, in the days when the Greeks ruled Israel, a Jewish merchant traveling in Greece was caught in a rainstorm. Shivering with cold, he saw a light up ahead. An inn! He would be able to dry himself off and warm himself up.

But in that inn were three Greeks, mean-spirited folks, indeed, who thought themselves much, much better than any mere Jew. And when they saw the Jewish merchant dare to enter the inn in which they sat, they were not happy at all. As he dried himself off before the fire, they muttered together.

"We cannot let this Jew sit in the same room with us," said one Greek.

"We must find a way to be rid of him," said the second Greek.

"I know!" exclaimed the third Greek. "We shall trick him into leaving the inn. And if he tries to get back in, why, we shall bolt the door!"

What the three Greeks didn't realize was that they were talking loudly enough for the merchant to overhear them.

"I am not going to be thrown back out into that cold, wet storm," he thought. "What's more, I think it's time you three hate-filled men were taught a little lesson!"

He smiled at them, but they only stared back at him, frowning. "We have agreed," they said, "that no man can stay in this inn with us unless he can pass a little test. He must be able to give three mighty jumps."

Of course they didn't mean to let the merchant stay in the inn even if he did pass their test, and the merchant knew it. He bowed his head meekly and said, "Oh dear. I'm afraid I don't know how to give a mighty jump. Perhaps you would be kind enough to show me?"

The Greeks burst into laughter. What a fool this Jew was! Imagine not even knowing how to jump! "Come," they said to each other, "we'll show him how to jump."

The first Greek gave a mighty jump and reached the middle of the inn.

"I can do better than that!" cried the second Greek. He gave a mightier jump and made it to the doorway.

The third Greek laughed. "Do you call that a jump? Watch this!"

He gave the mightiest jump of all, and landed in the courtyard outside.

When the first two Greeks rushed out to see where their friend had landed, the merchant calmly bolted the door behind them.

"Hey," they shouted, "let us back in!"

"I'm sorry. No."

"Let us in, we say! You've done a nasty thing."

But the merchant only smiled. "Oh, no," he said. "My friends, I've only done what you meant to do to me. Now good night to you!"

And he settled himself comfortably before the nice, warm fire.

The Master Thief

A FOLKTALE FROM TUNISIA

Once upon a time there lived a boy named Awad, whose dead father had been a thief. Awad's mother decided she wanted her son to learn a more honorable profession. She tried apprenticing him to a barber, but Awad stole the barber's razor. She tried apprenticing him to a carpenter, but Awad stole the carpenter's saw. At last Awad said to his mother, "What was my father's profession?"

She admitted, "He was a thief."

"Aha! Then I, too, want to be a thief," he replied.

So Awad became the apprentice of his uncle, who was a master thief. The boy learned all his lessons well. Then came the time for his final test.

Awad's uncle climbed a tree and stole the eggs right out from under a nesting bird.

"Now it is your turn, Awad. Return the eggs."

Awad scrambled up that tree and slipped the eggs back into the nest. The bird never even ruffled a feather.

Awad's uncle cheered. "Now you are a true thief! You shall be my partner."

So the two thieves went into business. They stole here and they stole there. Two things only they never did: they never stole from the poor, and they never hurt a soul.

Time went by. Awad and his uncle grew bored. "What shall we do now?" they wondered. "Let us rob the palace of the king!"

All went well the first night. They broke into the royal treasury and took away an armful of gold. All went well the second night also, when they broke into the royal treasury again and took away two armfuls of gold.

Alas, the king realized he was being robbed. His clever minister put a big barrel of boiling pitch right under the hole the thieves had made in the treasury roof. Awad's uncle fell into the barrel and died. In his uncle's honor, Awad took away three armfuls of gold—but he couldn't carry off his uncle's body as well.

In the morning, the king found the body of one thief, but since more treasure was missing, he knew another thief had escaped.

"Hang the body in the town square," advised the minister. "The other thief will surely try to rescue it."

Meanwhile, Awad, who had guessed the minister's plan, bought a flock of sheep with some of the gold from the royal treasury, and tied lit candles to their fleece. He drove them through the square in the middle of the night. The guards were sure these weird figures were ghost-thieves come to mourn their comrade, and they ran off in fright. Awad carried his uncle's body off for an honorable burial.

The next morning, the angry king asked his minister, "Now how do we catch the thief?"

"Hmm … " pondered the minister. "Ha, I have it! Put a jewelled collar on an ostrich and tie the ostrich to a long rope. Have a guard hold the other end of the rope. The thief will surely want the collar! When he tries to get it, the guard can catch him."

But Awad cut the rope so gently the guard never felt a thing. Awad and his mother ate the ostrich and kept the collar.

"That didn't work very well," the king shouted at his minister.

The minister sighed. "Scatter gold coins in the street," he suggested, "as though a strongbox had burst open. Set guards all around to catch whoever picks up the coins."

But Awad was too clever to be caught so easily. He used the jewels from the ostrich's collar to hire a caravan of camels. The saddlebags on their left sides he filled with flour; those on their right sides he filled with salt. Then he smeared their wide, flat feet with sticky soap.

"Look at that," said a guard standing on the camels' left sides. "A caravan carrying flour."

"Flour?" said a guard on the right-hand side. "They're carrying salt!"

"Flour!" cried the first guard.

"Salt!" cried the second guard.

While they argued back and forth, the sticky soap picked up every one of the coins.

"I give up," the minister said.

"So do I," added the king. "That thief is just too clever. In fact, I think I'd rather have such a clever fellow on my side."

He pardoned Awad and offered him the hand of his daughter in marriage. Awad took one look at the princess and fell madly in love with her, and she with him. And everyone, from thief to princess, lived happily—for a time.

Ah, but things weren't settled yet. The king of a neighboring land sent a mocking letter to Awad's father-in-law, taunting him about having surrendered to a thief. Awad's wife wept in shame.

"Don't weep," Awad begged her. "All will be well."

"But ... but how can it be?" she sobbed. "That king has mocked my father's honor!"

"Then I'll have to teach that king a lesson." Awad grinned. "When I'm done, I promise you he will bark like a dog, bray like a donkey, and crow like a rooster."

Off Awad went to the neighboring kingdom. He stole his way into the room right next to the king's bedroom, pulling a large wooden chest with him. Awad scraped away the dividing wall till it was as thin as paper. Then he called to the sleeping king in a grim, grim voice, "I have come for you."

The king woke with a cry of fear. "Who ... who are you?"

"I am the angel of death," Awad said. "I have come to take you to paradise."

With that, Awad broke through the wall. He was covered with white plaster dust from head to foot, and his eyes flashed wildly. "Enter this chest," he commanded the trembling king. "You shall be carried to paradise."

The king didn't want to leave the land of the living, but he certainly wanted to reach paradise, so he crawled meekly into the chest.

Awad quickly locked the chest. He brushed all the dust off himself and his plain clothes. Now he looked just like an ordinary servant. With the help of other servants, he had the chest loaded on a ship that carried Awad and the chest back home. Soon they were in the court of Awad's father-in-law.

"Before you may enter paradise," he told the king in the chest, "you must clean your soul."

"How ... how can I do that?" the king asked humbly.

"You must rid it of animal elements," Awad said. "To do that, you must bark like a dog, bray like a donkey, and crow like a rooster."

By now, the king was eager to get out of that hot, cramped chest. He barked, brayed, and crowed with all his might!

Awad laughed. "Now enter paradise!" he cried, and cast open the chest.

The king tumbled out, right in front of Awad's royal father-in-law and all his court. Everyone burst into laughter.

And what of the king? Well, at first he was furious at the trick that had been played on him. But he was so glad to be alive that after a moment, he, too, started to laugh.

"Forgive my rude letter," he told his neighbor king. "Now I can see why you want this clever young man as friend, not foe!"

And there was peace after that between the two countries.

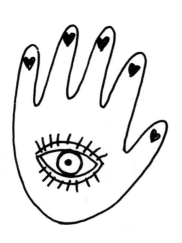

The Thankful Ghost

A FOLKTALE FROM EASTERN EUROPE

Once in the long ago days, Ari, a young Jewish merchant, was traveling in Turkey. There he saw a coffin hanging from a scaffold, watched over by the sultan's own guards.

"Why is someone being denied a burial?" the young man asked one of the guards.

"In that coffin is the body of one of the sultan's own advisors," the guard answered. He added in a whisper, "He was a good man, but he had enemies, and they convinced the sultan that he was a traitor. So the sultan won't let him be buried unless someone is willing to spend the money to ransom his body."

Ari felt sorry for the misjudged advisor. "I'll do it," he said, and paid for the body to be buried in sacred ground.

His business in Turkey completed, the young man set out for home. But as he was sailing back to the Holy Land, a terrible storm arose. Wild winds struck the ship and sank it. Ari was thrown into the raging ocean. Each time he tried to swim, the waves slapped him down, keeping him from air. At last he could fight no longer, and willed his soul to God.

But just as the young man was about to drown, a huge white eagle came swooping down out of the storm. Its mighty talons closed about Ari, and with one great surge, the eagle snatched the young man from the ocean. Ari gasped to see the water so far below him, and closed his eyes. But then he opened them again, just in time to see the water end and the land begin.

The eagle circled down and down, and gently dropped Ari safely on the ground. Then, as the young man stared, the eagle's shape blurred and turned into the form of a man in a white shroud.

"Who ... who are you?" Ari stammered.

"I am the ghost of he who was hung in chains," the figure told him. "I am he who was granted an honorable burial by your kindness. Now I have repaid that kindness. Fare you well, young man."

And with that, the ghost vanished into the air.

The Ghostly Congregation

A FOLKTALE FROM ROMANIA

Once there was an honest worker who had been laboring hard all day in the fields. He went to the evening service in the town synagogue, but was so tired he fell asleep in the middle of it.

The sound of music woke the worker. He looked sleepily about. It was the middle of the night, and moonlight was streaming into the synagogue through the open windows.

How strange! He could see by the light of the moon that the congregation still seemed to be here, and that they were dancing. But the music sounded so eerie ... and why weren't any lamps lit? Why was everyone dressed in the same flowing white robes?

All of a sudden, the man realized that they weren't robes—they were burial shrouds. This was a gathering of ghosts!

He sprang up from his bench with a shout of horror and raced for the door, but a cold, cold hand pulled him back. The worker tore free and ran to the window, yelling for help till the whole village was awakened. The rabbi and a minyan (the ritual number of men needed for prayer) hurried into the synagogue and pulled the worker safely out, back to the world of the living.

What happened to the ghosts? No one knows. But no one in that village ever slept in the synagogue again!

The Insulted Ghosts

A FOLKTALE FROM THE TALMUD

Once, long, long ago, Yesef the farmer had a fight with his wife, Leah. What was it about? What many such fights are about: something silly. Yesef had given one gold coin to a beggar. Leah told him he should have given two silver coins. Different coins, the same amount. But husband and wife argued about it and argued about it, and by the time the fight was over, Yesef had no place to spend the night but in the cemetery.

"At least it will be nice and quiet here," he muttered.

But as Yesef settled down to sleep, the quiet was broken by voices. Who was speaking so late in a cemetery? Ghosts! Yesef was overhearing two girl-ghosts.

"Come out," the first ghost said to the second. "Let's go flying over the land and hear what living people say. And let's see what the future holds for them."

"You go," the second ghost said. "My shroud's such an ugly thing. I'd be ashamed if anyone saw me in it. Go, and tell me what you see."

Off the first ghost flew. The hours passed. At last she returned.

"Oh, such mischief!" she told the other girl-ghost. "There's going to be a hailstorm very soon."

"A hailstorm?"

"Yes, and if anyone sows his fields too early, the storm will destroy his crop."

Yesef waited until the girl-ghosts had settled down for the night, then tiptoed back to his house. When the day came for sowing crops, he only sat at home.

"What's wrong with you?" Leah scolded. "Why aren't you working?"

"I will," he soothed. "Only wait a bit."

He sowed his crops a good month after everyone else, when their fields were already full of ripening grain. Sure enough, just as the girl-ghost had predicted, a terrible hailstorm struck. And since none of Yesef's crops had started to sprout, his were the only crops safe beneath the ground.

A year passed. Yesef began to wonder what new things the girl-ghosts might predict. So off he went one night to the cemetery, where sure enough, he heard the girl-ghosts talking again.

"Come on!" the first one urged, just as she had a year ago. "Let's go hear what the living people are saying, and let's see what the future holds for them."

"No!" the second ghost said. "You know I don't want anyone to see me in my ugly old shroud."

So off the first ghost flew. When she finally returned, she reported to the second girl-ghost, "Oh, what mischief! I learned that the summer is going to be very hot. Anyone who plants his crops too late is going to have them burned by the sun."

Yesef tiptoed home. To Leah's surprise, he planted his crops in the early spring, long before anyone else.

"Have you gone mad?" she cried.

"Watch and wait," Yesef replied, sitting comfortably in front of their house. "Watch and wait."

Sure enough, the summer was very hot, indeed. Yesef was the only farmer who had crops ready to be harvested before everyone else's crops were burned by the sun.

Now, by this time Leah's curiosity was beginning to itch her. Where was Yesef getting this sudden wisdom of his?

"Lucky guesses," Yesef told her.

"Humph!" Leah exclaimed. "You never made such lucky guesses before. No, someone has been telling you all this, someone very wise. Who is it?"

Well, Yesef didn't want to tell her. He didn't want to risk doing anything that might keep him from learning the future. But the longer he refused to speak, the angrier Leah grew. At last she cried, "You never tell me anything! You don't really love me."

Yesef sighed. He did love Leah, even when she scolded him. "All right," he said. "Come with me. I'll show you."

That night, he took her to the cemetery. Leah gasped in wonder when the two girl-ghosts started talking.

"Come on!" the first ghost cried. "Let's go flying and hear what the living people say."

But the second ghost snapped, "Let's stay right her and keep our mouths shut. Someone's been eavesdropping on us. In fact, someone's eavesdropping right now!"

Both girl-ghosts began to sink back into their graves.

"I tell you," said one of them, just before they disappeared, "the world has come to a pretty pass. There's no such thing as privacy any more!"

The Restless Ghost

A FOLKTALE FROM POLAND

Once, in the fine old Polish city of Cracow, a sickly fellow went to the Jewish cemetery.

"Caretaker," he said, coughing weakly, "I would like to buy a cemetery plot."

"Well, I can sell you one," the caretaker said. "How about over there, out by the far wall?"

The sickly man shook his head. "No, that is a pauper's grave. I have been a simple man all my life, but I do have one great dream. I wish to be buried in the plot next to the late rabbi—on his head be peace—himself."

Alas, the caretaker was a crooked soul. The plot next to the late rabbi was a very expensive one. "There are no witnesses here," he told himself. "No one will be able to prove which plot I've sold."

So he took the sickly man's money. But of course if anyone ever asked, he meant to deny he'd ever sold that expensive plot. Then he could sell it all over again!

The very next day, the sickly man died. The caretaker buried him in the pauper's grave by the far wall.

But that night, while the caretaker slept, a cold, cold voice asked, "Where is my grave?"

To the caretaker's horror, the sickly man stood before him, eyes glowing with an eerie light. "Where is my grave?" the ghost repeated.

"You … you have a grave!" the caretaker stammered.

But the ghost only repeated yet again, "Where is my grave? You have stolen my grave."

As the ghost moved towards him, the caretaker let out a great yell of fright, and the ghost vanished.

"I … I must have been dreaming," the caretaker told himself, mopping his brow.

But the next night, the ghost returned.

"Where is my grave?" he asked. "Give me my grave."

And so things went, night after night. Soon the caretaker didn't dare go to bed, didn't dare fall asleep! Trembling and weary, he finally knew he must confess what he had done.

So the caretaker went to the town rabbi. "I have committed a terrible crime," he began, and told the rabbi everything.

"No wonder that poor ghost is unhappy!" the rabbi exclaimed. "You are keeping him from his rest. You took his money and made him a promise, and a promise is not to be broken."

"But … but what can I do now?"

"When the ghost next appears to you, tell him he may move into the plot he bought."

So the caretaker did just that. The next morning, he started off to the cemetery to make arrangements for the sickly man's body to be moved into the right plot. But when the caretaker arrived, he gave a yell of surprise.

A new grave was already there in the plot by the late rabbi's grave, even though no living soul had dug it.

And the restless ghost was seen no more.

The Gilgul

A FOLKTALE FROM POLAND

What is a gilgul? Some people say it is the spirit of someone who was once alive but hasn't quite decided to leave the world of the living. Every now and then, the stories say, a gilgul may decide to try to move into the body of someone else.

One day, long ago, little Sophie, a happy, healthy girl, went into the woods to gather mushrooms with her friends. But she had no sooner opened her mouth to cough when— zip! Just like that, a gilgul had taken up housekeeping in her body. As soon as the gilgul got used to being in a living body once more, it began ordering poor Sophie about. Her family all wondered at the change in her.

And what a change it was! Where once Sophie had been happy, now she was always gloomy. Where before she had been polite and well-behaved, now she was rough and noisy.

But the gilgul soon grew bored. It didn't want to spend its time locked up in the body of a little girl. It had better things to do! So the gilgul let the family know it was there.

"I am a gilgul," it cried in Sophie's voice, "and I want, I *demand* to see the rabbi!"

Well, what could the family do? They lived out in the forest, and the rabbi lived in town. They didn't want to go all that way, or bother him at his holy studies. So Sophie's old grandfather said, "I will pretend to be the rabbi. The gilgul will never know the difference."

But before he could even order the spirit to leave poor Sophie alone, the gilgul burst into rough laughter.

"You, a rabbi? You?" it cried. "You're the one who started all this fuss—you ordered my tree cut down."

This didn't make any sense to the family at all. "Your pardon," Sophie's father began, "but what tree? Who … what … who are you?"

The gilgul sighed. "Foolish people! I was once a man. But I died without anyone saying kaddish, the proper funeral prayers, over me, so my spirit stayed right here among the living. Where could I go? If I didn't find myself a body, I might be lost forever, so I entered the first living thing I saw: a dog.

But mean boys killed the dog. Then I entered a horse, but the horse died. This was in the middle of the forest, and there wasn't anything else around except trees, so I entered a tree. And there I was, living very nicely. But you had the tree cut down! There wasn't anyplace else for me to go but into the body of this little girl. I don't want to stay here, and you don't want me to be here—so someone call the rabbi!"

This time the family agreed. They sent for the rabbi. When he heard what had happened, he agreed to give the proper services for the dead.

As soon as the rabbi had finished, the gilgul cried out, "At last!" and with a wild shout and a rush of wind, it happily vanished.

The Poet and His Servant

A FOLKTALE FROM SPAIN

Once, many long years ago, the poet Solomon ibn Gabirol lived in the city of Valencia. Now, Solomon was a clever man, almost as wise as the legendary King Solomon of Israel. When he wasn't working on his verses, he was pondering problems in philosophy or science.

But all this poetry-writing and pondering didn't allow Solomon much time for anything else. One day he looked around his dusty, messy house and said, "I need a servant!"

Now, anyone else would go to the market and hire someone. Not Solomon!

"What good is all my studying if I can't make a servant for myself?"

So Solomon shut himself up in his house with a pile of earth and all his books. What he did, how he did it, no one knows. But when Solomon finally came out of that house, he was no longer alone. With him was a woman, a maidservant as blank-faced as stone and plain as earth. She cleaned and cooked and sewed for Solomon without a single word of complaint—or any word at all—and the happy poet was left to write his verses and think his thoughts in peace.

But he forgot about his neighbors.

"Did you see the poet's new servant?" they whispered. "She never talks, or laughs, or sings. She won't even answer our greetings!"

"Maybe she is a foreigner," someone said.

"But her eyes are so blank," someone else said. "There's nothing in there, no sense, no life."

"No soul!" the neighbors cried as one.

They were overheard by a merchant. When he went to the market, he whispered to all his fellow merchants, "Have you heard the news? The poet Solomon has a soulless demon for a servant!"

He was overheard by a guard. When he went to the royal palace, he whispered to all his fellow guards, "Have you heard the news? The poet Solomon has been dealing with demons!"

He was overheard by the king's prime minister. The minister rushed to the king and cried, "The poet Solomon is a sorcerer! He's been calling up demons!"

"Demons!" the king cried. "We can't have my people in danger from demons. Order this sorcerer-poet to come before me."

So the puzzled Solomon found himself being dragged by palace guards before the king.

"You stand accused of practicing the Dark Arts, working sorcery, and raising demons!" the king thundered. "How do you plead?"

"Not guilty, Your Majesty!" Solomon gasped.

Tales of Ghosts and Other Strange Things 93

"But everyone has seen your captive demon," the minister argued.

"My ... oh, you mean my servant!" Solomon tried to laugh. But the king and his minister looked so fierce that the laugh died away. "If you'll only let me bring it here, I'll show you the truth of the matter."

So Solomon brought the blank-eyed maidservant before the royal court. "You see?" he said. "This isn't a demon or a living woman. It's only a ... a golem, a thing I created out of earth, to help with the cleaning. I'm ... uh ... I'm a sloppy housekeeper," he added.

But no one believed him, not the king, not the minister. With a sigh, Solomon said certain words and made certain gestures. His servant sank back into a little mound of harmless earth.

The king was satisfied. His minister was satisfied. The guards and merchants and neighbors were satisfied. Solomon was not a sorcerer. He was not calling up demons.

Only Solomon wasn't happy. He didn't dare create another golem, not after all that fuss! And so he had to do all the dusting and cooking and sewing for himself.

The Golem of Prague

A FOLKTALE FROM CZECHOSLOVAKIA

Once, long ago in the city of Prague, some people hated the Jews who lived in that city. Why? Jews and Christians both worship the same God, but they worship in different ways. Those wicked people hated the Jews just because they weren't Christians. And so they began to spread terrible rumors that the Jews of Prague were murdering Christian children. Of course this wasn't true, but when people are afraid, they believe even the strangest rumors.

The chief rabbi of Prague, a wise and wonderworking man known as the Maharal, was worried for his congregation. Surely it was just a matter of time before fear turned to violence. Surely the Jews needed a guardian!

So the holy Maharal went down to the river with his two apprentices. Out of the clay of the river's bank they formed the figure of a gigantic man. The Maharal spoke words from the Holy Scriptures over it, and the clay figure, the golem, opened his eyes.

"Stand," the Maharal told him.

The golem stood. The three men dressed him, and took him back with them to Prague.

"But ... but we can't tell anyone what he really is!" one apprentice said. "People would think he was a monster."

"No one shall know," the Maharal agreed. He told the golem, "You are Joseph. And you will serve me even if I tell you to jump into fire."

The golem, being only a thing of clay, could not speak, but he nodded obediently.

The Maharal added firmly, "Your purpose in being is to protect the Jews of Prague from harm."

Again the golem nodded obediently.

The Maharal brought the golem to his home, where everyone took Joseph to be no more than a poor, weak-witted servant. Even the Maharal's own wife, Perele, believed it. One day she asked Joseph to fill the water barrels—but she forgot to tell him to stop! The golem kept on bringing bucket after bucket of water, till the Maharal's house was nearly flooded.

"Why do you keep such a foolish servant?" Perele angrily asked her husband.

"He will prove his worth," the Maharal assured her.

And of course the Maharal was right. When evil men threatened the Jews, Joseph patrolled the streets like a huge, silent soldier. Again and again he saved the Jews from anyone who tried to hurt them.

The people who hated the Jews were furious. They would not let any huge, silent soldier stop them! So they decided on a terribly cruel plot. They went to the Christian cemetery and dug up the body of a boy.

"We'll hide it in the home of the Maharal himself," they decided. "Then we will call in the guards. Everyone will believe the Jews have been murdering Christian children, and that will be the end of the Jews of Prague!"

But even as they plotted, not one of those hate-filled people realized that Joseph was following them like a giant, silent shadow. Just before they were about to throw the boy's body into the Maharal's house, the golem caught them. He scooped them all up in his mighty arms, carried them to the house of the city's watchman, and dropped them all right in the courtyard.

The noise woke the watchman and his neighbors. They came running and found the grave robbers and the boy's body. Once the watchman learned of the plot, he hurried to the palace to tell Prague's ruler, King Rudolf.

"What a horrible thing!" the king exclaimed. "But how fortunate we all are that these cruel people were stopped in time!"

And he issued a royal decree on the spot: None of his people was ever again to spread rumors about the Jews, on pain of banishment.

Life grew peaceful for the Jews of Prague after that. When a whole year had passed without trouble, the Maharal knew the golem was no longer needed. He led Joseph to the attic, where the Maharal and his apprentices spoke holy and magical words over him.

When they were finished, the golem was no more than lifeless clay. The Maharal hid the clay under a pile of old papers and books.

"Sleep well, Joseph," he murmured.

And who knows? For all anyone can tell, the golem is sleeping there still, waiting for the time when he will be needed once more.

Doing the Right Thing

A Good Deed Repaid

A FOLKTALE FROM THE TALMUD

Once, long years ago, there lived the famous Rabbi Akiba. Now, the good rabbi had a daughter he dearly loved. Oh, but how horrible! The astrologers all told him that on his daughter's wedding day, she would be bitten by a snake and die. What could he do? How could he protect her? Should he keep his daughter unwed and lonely? No, no, that was surely not the right thing to do, because she had already met and fallen in love with a young man.

So the wedding day arrived. As the guests sat happily at the wedding feast, a poor, ragged beggar came to the door. No one wanted to pay him any notice, because no one wanted to leave the celebrating.

But the rabbi's daughter saw the sad, lonely beggar. She left her place to bring him some food and drink. As she walked, the pretty clasp holding back her hair came loose. She impatiently pulled it free and stuck it into a crack in the wall, meaning to recover it later. But in all the excitement of her wedding day, she forgot all about it.

The next day, the rabbi's daughter finally remembered her hair clasp. She pulled it out of the crack in the wall—and screamed. Oh, how frightening! A poisonous snake tumbled out of the wall as well.

Everyone came running to kill the snake, but it was already dead. On her wedding day, when she had stuck the clasp into the crack, the rabbi's daughter had accidentally stabbed the snake that had been poised to strike her.

Rabbi Akiba sighed with relief. By his daughter's act of pure kindness towards a beggar, she had overcome the strength of the prophesy and saved herself from a painful death.

One Gold Coin

A FOLKTALE FROM EASTERN EUROPE

Once, long ago, a poor man went to the synagogue to pray. On his way there, he found a pile of gold coins lying in the street—but it was the Sabbath, the weekly day of prayer during which observant Jews are not allowed to handle money. Being a pious man, he didn't touch so much as a coin. When the Sabbath was over, someone else had taken the gold, leaving behind only one gold coin. With a sigh, the poor man took it home and gave it to his wife.

Now, in that same town there lived a wealthy merchant named Simon. Simon was just about to set sail on a trading voyage to far-off lands when the poor man's wife came up to him.

"Please, sir," she said shyly, "I have only one gold coin. But oh, I would so love to have something from far away. Would you buy me something with this coin?"

Simon took her coin with a polite bow. "Of course," he told her.

But the voyage was long, and took Simon to many strange lands. He completely forgot about the poor woman's coin until he was ready to set sail for home.

"Ah, wait for me," he cried, hurrying back ashore.

"We can't wait too long," the ship's captain called to him. "The wind will fail!"

So Simon decided to buy the first thing he saw—and what did he see but a beggar carrying three young cats in a sack.

"Where are you going with those cats?" Simon asked.

"I have no use for them, and I can't afford to feed them," the beggar replied. "So I'm going to drown them."

"No," Simon cried, "don't be so cruel! Wait, I'll buy them from you."

He searched in his purse. But the only coin he had left after all his trading was the one belonging to the poor woman. Simon gave it to the beggar and went back aboard the ship with the three cats.

Off the ship sailed. But alas, the good, strong wind that drove it along all too soon grew into a terrible storm. Simon and his three cats were swept overboard by a mighty wave.

They were cast ashore with nothing worse than a good wetting. But the shore on which they landed was a country of savage people who hated strangers. When they caught a stranger, why, they locked him up in a house that swarmed with mice. (Indeed, all of their village swarmed with mice!) The stranger would be left locked up with the mice until they ate him.

But Simon had his cats with him. As soon as the door was closed and locked, he let the three of them loose, and they soon put an end to all the mice.

In the morning, the savage people came to see what had happened to the stranger. To their surprise, they found Simon alive and unhurt, his three cats purring happily by his side. There wasn't a mouse to be seen.

The savage people had never seen a cat before. They thought these three mouse-killing cats were the most amazing, most wonderful creatures in the world.

"What do you call these marvelous beasts?" they asked.

"Cats," Simon told them.

"We must have these cats!" the people cried. "Will you take a sack of gold for them?"

"Well ... " Simon pretended to hesitate.

"Two sacks?"

"I don't know ... "

"Three sacks!" they cried. "Three whole sacks of gold for your cats!"

Simon agreed. The crew of his ship had been looking for him, and he quickly hurried aboard with his gold.

This time there were no storms. Safely home, Simon counted up all his profits and smiled. Even with that storm, it had been a good voyage!

But then he remembered the poor woman and her one gold coin.

"Without that coin, I wouldn't be alive," he told his servants, and went to see the poor husband and wife.

"Where did you get your gold coin?" he asked the woman.

"From my husband," she answered nervously.

"And where did *you* get it?" Simon asked the man.

The poor man sighed and told how he'd found the pile of gold coins but hadn't touched it because of his reverence for the Sabbath. Simon nodded. "Was the pile of gold this big?" he asked, and emptied one of his sacks of gold onto the floor. "Or perhaps this big?" he added, emptying the second sack. "Ah, I know—it must have been this big!"

With that, he emptied the third sack of gold onto the floor. Happily, Simon went his way, leaving the poor man and woman poor no longer.

The Two Beggars

A FOLKTALE FROM AFGHANISTAN

Once upon a time, there were two beggars who passed under one of the windows of the royal palace every day. Every day, the sultan would toss coins down to them. Each time he did, he heard one beggar cry, "Blessings upon the head of the sultan! He is a fountain of kindness, a wonder of charity!"

But each time, the other beggar said only, "Praise be to God for His kindness."

Hearing this, the sultan grew angry.

"*I* give you the coins," he shouted down at the beggar, "and yet you never praise me—you always thank someone else!"

"I thank God," the beggar answered quietly. "Your Majesty, I really do appreciate your charity. But were it not for the kindness of God, you would not be able to be so generous to us."

"Humph!" the sultan said. "I don't believe a word of that. You are only a foolish beggar, not a wise man." But how could he prove the beggar wrong? The sultan hurried to the royal bakery and told the baker, "I want you to prepare two loaves of bread. They are to be identical in every way."

The baker did as the sultan commanded. The sultan carefully cut a hole in one loaf, scooped out some of the bread, packed the loaf full of jewels, and closed up the hole again. Once again, the two loaves looked exactly the same.

The next day, when the beggars passed under his window, he gave the beggar who thanked only God the plain loaf. But he gave the loaf stuffed with jewels to the beggar who praised only the sultan.

"Now we'll see who is thanked," the sultan said to himself.

But as the two beggars left the palace, the beggar who praised only the sultan noticed that his loaf of bread seemed heavier than it should be.

"It must be badly baked," he decided, but he didn't tell this to the other beggar. Instead, all he said was, "You like your bread more thoroughly baked. Why don't we switch loaves?"

The other beggar, suspecting nothing, agreed.

Ah, but when he went to eat his loaf, he found the jewels inside! Now he was truly thankful to God because he no longer needed to beg for a living.

The next day, the sultan was amazed to find only one beggar under his window—the beggar who always praised the sultan. "What did you do with the loaf I gave you yesterday?" the sultan asked.

The beggar hung his head. "It was hard," he muttered. "I didn't think it was well-baked. So I traded it for the other beggar's loaf."

Now at last the sultan understood what the beggar who thanked God had been trying to tell him.

"Riches really do come only from God," he said.

Throwing Stones

A FOLKTALE FROM THE TALMUD

Once, long ago, there lived a rich man who was never satisfied. His mansion was large and splendid and his gardens were cool and beautiful. But it was never good enough for him. No, he was always insisting that his servants add a wall here, or dig a new garden there.

As the servants dug, they uncovered a good many rocks.

"Master, what shall we do with all these stones?" they asked.

"Oh, just throw them over the walls out onto the public road," he said.

One day a wise old man walked down that road. He saw the servants tossing stones out onto it, and asked, "Why are you doing that?"

"Our master commanded it," they told him.

So the wise old man went up to the rich man and asked, "Why do you throw stones from yours to not yours?"

That didn't mean much to the rich man. "All I want to do is get all these stones off my estate."

"But this is a public road. What about all the people who have to walk on it?"

The rich man shrugged. "Why should I care what happens to them?"

"I think you will learn to regret what you've just said," the wise old man murmured, and went on his way.

Sure enough, things went from bad to worse for the rich man after that. All his investments failed, and money slipped through his fingers no matter how hard he tried to grasp it. At last he was beggared, and thrown out of his lovely estate. As the once rich man wandered the public road, his feet were bruised by the very stones he had ordered his servants to toss out.

"Now I know what the wise old man meant," he said sadly. "Now I'm truly sorry I threw stones from mine to not mine!"

Which Was the Truly Pious?

A FOLKTALE FROM EASTERN EUROPE

Once, or so the tale is told, three men happened to die at the same time, and their souls went up to heaven. As they approached the wonderful, golden gates of heaven, however, they were stopped by the recording angel. He was very tall and very thin and dressed all in spotless white robes. His face looked as though it had never smiled. In his arms, he held a huge book in which was written down everything the three souls had done while they were alive.

"Approach," he told the three souls. "Tell me who you were in life. Then tell me why you should be allowed to enter heaven."

The first soul stepped forward. "I was a rabbi," he said. "Night and day I proved how much I knew of the law. Night and day I studied only the Holy Word. And so I deserve a place in heaven."

The soul started towards the gates, but the recording angel stopped him. "Not so fast. First we must look into the reason behind all your studying. We must learn whether you were studying for honor, or just for wealth."

The second soul stepped forward. "I was a pious man in life," he said. "I fasted all the time. I observed every religious obligation every day of my life. And so I deserve a place in heaven."

The soul started towards the gates, but the recording angel stopped him. "Not so fast. First we must look into the reason behind all your piety. We must learn whether you were being pious for the sake of holiness, or just out of self-pride."

The third soul had been hiding shyly behind the other two. Now he came meekly forward, head bowed before the recording angel. "I wasn't a rabbi or anything as wonderful as that," he began. "I tried to keep all the holy days, but … well … I didn't always have the time. You see, I was only an innkeeper when I was alive."

"And what did you do while you were an innkeeper?" the recording angel asked.

The soul thought for a long, long time. Finally he said humbly, "My door was always open to those in need."

The stern face of the recording angel burst into a smile. He stepped aside as the gates of heaven swung open. "Enter," he said. "We need no further study here!"

The Trapper Trapped

A FOLKTALE FROM POLAND

Once upon a time, a poor clerk stole a little money from the merchant who employed him so he could hire a doctor for his pregnant wife.

The merchant was furious. "Why should I care if his wife is going to have a baby? He stole from me, and no one ever dares steal from me. I shall have my revenge on that clerk, come what may!"

So the merchant waited until the clerk's wife gave birth to a son. Then the merchant sent a man to steal the baby. He placed it in a chest, and threw the chest under a bridge.

"There," he said, "now I have my revenge."

But a fisherman who lived in a hut near the bridge saw the chest fall. Curious, he went to see what might be in it, and inside he found the baby, frightened but unharmed.

The fisherman gave a cry of joy. He and his wife had always longed for a child of their own, and now heaven had granted them a son. He hurried home with the baby, which he and his wife named Yankl. Together, they raised Yankl with love.

The years passed. Yankl the baby grew into Yankl the fine young man. One day the merchant who had stolen that baby happened to see him. Now, of course the merchant couldn't know that this was the baby he had stolen. All he saw was an intelligent young fellow. So he hired Yankl and set him to work in his shop.

Yankl proved himself both clever and kind. In fact, so pleased was the merchant with the young man's progress that he decided Yankl would make a fine heir. Yes, the young man and his own daughter should be wed! Off the merchant went to talk to the fisherman.

Well, one thing led to another. Soon the merchant and the fisherman were chatting away like old friends. At last the fisherman confessed to the merchant that Yankl, fine young man though he was, wasn't really his son at all.

"No, I found him as a baby."

"You ... found him?"

"Why, yes," the fisherman said. "He was in a chest someone had tossed off a bridge!"

The merchant was stunned. His daughter marry the son of the thieving clerk? Never! He wrote a letter to his wife, saying, "Yankl must never marry our daughter. You must hire someone to kill him!"

Sealing the letter, he smiled falsely at Yankl and handed it to him. "Take this to my wife, if you would," the merchant said. "You will be well rewarded."

Yankl, of course, suspected nothing. Off he went to the merchant's wife. But it was a long journey, and by the time he arrived it was late at night.

"It wouldn't be polite to wake the merchant's wife," he decided. "I'll sleep here in the synagogue tonight, and give her the letter in the morning."

But as Yankl slept, the letter fell out of his pocket. The seal broke open. The rabbi picked it up, meaning to give it back to the young man, but the words "kill him!" caught the wise man's eye. He read the whole letter and frowned. Tearing the letter to bits, he wrote a second letter instead, asking the merchant's wife to welcome the young man properly, and stuck it into Yankl's pocket.

Time passed. The merchant returned home. What was this? Not only was Yankl still alive, he and the merchant's daughter had fallen deeply in love!

"No, this can't be! He must die."

The merchant could think of nothing else. Night and day, day and night, he tried to find a way to kill Yankl.

At last an idea struck him. Late one night, he stole out of the house and dug a deep pit right in front of the main door to the house.

"When Yankl comes out in the morning, he will fall right into the pit and die," he thought to himself.

So it surely would have been, but the next morning, even as Yankl had his hand on the doorknob of the front door, he thought he heard the merchant's daughter calling him from the back yard. So he left by the back door instead. The merchant saw him go, and gasped in shock.

"How can this be? How could he have suspected? Didn't I hide the pit well enough? If anyone else sees it, they'll know I tried to kill him!"

The merchant went rushing out to check the pit, tripped on the doorsill, and fell right into his own trap. That was the end of him, but Yankl and his love lived happily ever after.

Faith

A FOLKTALE FROM IRAN

Once, long ago, there lived a rich man named Abdallah. Now, though Abdallah had everything he wanted, he had lost his faith in God. One day Abdallah went to market with a bag of money, planning to give it to the first beggar who admitted that he, too, had lost his faith.

However, no matter how long Abdallah searched, he couldn't find one beggar who would admit he had lost his faith. Finally, he found the poorest beggar of all. So poor was this beggar that all he had to wear was a dirty old rag and all he had to sleep on was a bed of ashes.

"Surely *you* have lost your faith," Abdallah said.

But the beggar shook his head. "No matter how terrible my life may become, I shall never stop believing in God's help. Anyone who holds fast to his faith is always rewarded."

Abdallah gave up. Frustrated, he stormed out of the marketplace and went to the cemetery.

"Surely the dead have lost all hope!" he cried.

He buried the bag of money under a tombstone and went his way.

But hard times lay ahead. Abdallah's business failed, and after paying all his debts, he found he had nothing left. He wandered the road, begging for charity. At last, nearly starving, Abdallah prayed for help, and suddenly he remembered that bag of money he had buried in the cemetery. He hurried off to the cemetery and began to dig.

Alas, no sooner had he closed his hand around the bag of money than the cemetery guards caught him. Abdallah was dragged before the king to be sentenced as a robber.

"But I'm not a robber!" Abdallah protested. He stammered out his whole story, ending with, "In the name of the Lord, have pity on me."

"In the name of the Lord, I shall," the king replied. "Guards, release this man. Return his money to him." He studied Abdallah. "You don't recognize me, do you?"

"N–no, Your Majesty."

"I was that beggar you found sleeping on the bed of ashes. I told you then that I would never stop believing in God's help. Sure enough, help came! I was recognized as the lost heir to the throne, and here I am, beggar no longer."

Abdallah shook his head in wonder. "You were right, and I was wrong," he said. "He who holds fast to his faith always *is* rewarded."

Cake

A FOLKTALE FROM TUNISIA

Once upon a time there lived a selfish miser. So selfish was he that he never gave anything away unless it was so damaged he couldn't use it himself.

One day, that miser bought himself a nice piece of cake. But before he could so much as taste it, he dropped the cake in the street. When he picked it up, the miser gave a cry of disgust, for the cake was covered with dirt.

Just then, a poor man timidly asked the miser for charity. The miser never gave good coins away—instead, he handed the beggar the dirty piece of cake.

Ah, but that night, the miser had a strange, strange dream. In the dream, he was sitting in a large restaurant. It was a fine place, richly furnished, and it was also very crowded, with waiters running here and there. The miser's mouth began to water as he saw that the waiters were bringing people the most wonderful cakes he had ever seen.

Yet not one waiter came his way.

"Hey!" he called. "Service!"

At last a waiter came close enough to throw a piece of dirty cake onto his table.

"Come back here!" the miser roared. "This cake is filthy. How dare you serve it to me?"

The waiter only shrugged. "I'm sorry, sir. I'm only following orders."

"What nonsense! I didn't ask for charity—I have enough money to buy every cake in this restaurant!"

"No, sir, I'm afraid you don't," the waiter replied. "You can't use money here. You see, sir, this is eternity. Here you can only eat what you, yourself, sent ahead from the mortal world. You, alas, sent only this one dirty piece of cake, this one sorry bit of charity, in your whole life. And that, I'm afraid, is all you may receive."

The Good Neighbor

A FOLKTALE FROM MIDDLE EUROPE

Once, long ago in France, the king decided to banish all the Jews who lived in Paris. Why did he do this? It was a cruel whim. He gave the Jews only two days to get ready to leave.

Now, on one street in Paris lived two merchants who bought and sold jewels. One merchant was Jewish and one was Christian, but that difference had never mattered to them. They were good friends.

When the Jewish merchant learned he had been banished, he cried to his neighbor, "What shall I do? I can't carry all my jewels with me, but I can't just abandon them, either!"

"Leave them with me," the Christian merchant told him. "The king will change his mind soon enough and allow Jews back into the city. I swear to you before God that I will keep your jewels safe for you."

So the Jewish merchant agreed, and fled the city.

Long years passed. At last the cruel king died. When his son took the throne, one of the first things he did was declare that the Jews could return to Paris.

The Jewish merchant went home, afraid of what he would find. Could he trust his friend? Would any of his jewels be left?

But when he reached that friend's house, the Jewish merchant stared in horror. Where his friend's prosperous shop had been, there was nothing but a boarded-up doorway, and the house in which the shop once stood was nothing more than a ruin.

"What has happened?" he cried.

His friend heard him and came out of the ruin, dressed in worn, shabby clothing. "Not long after you left," the Christian merchant said, "there was a fire in my shop. I lost nearly everything. I've been a poor man ever since."

"But ... but you had my jewels!" the Jewish merchant told him. "Why didn't you use them to help yourself?"

"Ah, my friend," the Christian replied, "how could I betray you? I had sworn a sacred vow to keep them safe, and safe they are. I've hidden them in the cellar."

The Jewish merchant quickly set up shop again. He shared his wealth with his faithful neighbor, and the Jew and the Christian lived as brothers once more.

The Wise Men of Chelm

About the Wise Men of Chelm

FOLKTALES FROM EASTERN EUROPE

Why are there so many foolish folks in Chelm?
Once upon a time, one story says, when God was filling up the world with people, He gave an angel the job of delivering two sacks full of souls. One sack held the souls of all the wise people who were to be born in the world. The other sack held all the foolish souls. Wise and foolish souls were to be mixed together, the way they are in every other place.

But alas, the sacks were very heavy. As the angel was flying over Chelm, he didn't fly quite high enough. One of those sacks caught on the peak of a mountain and was ripped open.

And all the foolish souls fell out and landed right in Chelm!

Well, that's one story. But other people say that the folks of Chelm really aren't fools at all; no, it's just that foolish things keep happening to them!

Catching the Moon

It all started one dark, moonless night, a night so dark that the people of Chelm began to worry. What if someone went for a walk outside? If he forgot his lantern, or if the wind blew out the flame, he wouldn't be able to see where he was going!

"He could get lost," said Yussel the baker.

"He could fall down and hurt himself," added Hershel the miller.

"He could even be eaten by wild animals," cried Chaim the carpenter.

Everyone gasped. Eaten by wild animals! Oh no, that would never do. The people of Chelm thought and puzzled, puzzled and thought. The night was never dark when the moon was in the sky. But the moon didn't shine every night. What could they do?

"I have it!" said Hershel suddenly.

He told his plan to all the people. They nodded happily, and when the moon next shone in the sky, the people of Chelm were ready. They dragged out a big barrel of water into the village square and set it right under the moon.

Hershel stood on tiptoe and looked into the barrel. He gave a joyful laugh.

"It worked," he laughed joyfully. "The moon is trapped in there!"

Quickly the people of Chelm brought wood and nails and hammers. They nailed the wood down over the mouth of the barrel till not even a crack could be seen.

"We've done it!" they cried. "We've captured the moon. Now all we need to do is wait till the night is very dark, open the barrel, and let the moon shine out."

The next night, the sky was covered by clouds. It was very dark.

"Hurry," Hershel called. "Now's the time to let out the moon!"

The people of Chelm rushed out of their houses to where the covered barrel sat in the village square. Carefully they pulled off every nail and every piece of wood covering the barrel, but not even the faintest ray of moonlight shone out. Hershel stood on tiptoe and peeked into the barrel.

"No!" he gasped. "Oh no! The moon is gone!"

The people of Chelm tipped over the barrel and let the water spill out. They searched through every drop. But none of them could find even the smallest sliver of light.

Sadly, the people of Chelm sat down together in the village square. "It's no use," they said. "Someone must have stolen the moon."

Just then, the clouds parted. Moonlight poured down. The people of Chelm stared up, and one by one they started to laugh.

"What a wonderful thing!" they cried. "Someone may have stolen the moon, but it has escaped them. And there it is, back in the sky where it belongs!"

The Rock

O nce the people of Chelm were satisfied that the moon was back up in the sky where it belonged, they were free to worry about other things.

"There's that hill right outside town," Yussel the baker said one day.

"What about it?" everyone asked.

"Did you ever take a good look at the rock that sits on top of that hill?"

So off everyone went to take a good look at the rock. They all agreed it was a fine, big rock indeed.

"Yes, but what if someday it came loose?" Yussel asked. "What if it should fall? Why, it might fall right on our town!"

"It might break my millstone!" cried Hershel the miller.

"It might crush my woodwork!" yelled Chaim the carpenter.

"It might destroy our whole town!" Yussel added. "We had better do something about this."

So the wise men of Chelm worried and thought, thought and worried. At last they came up with a solution.

"We shall bring that rock down by ourselves," they declared.

But how could that be done? Again the wise men of Chelm worried and thought, thought and worried.

"We will all work together," they decided.

And so everyone who lived in Chelm—men and women, boys and girls—climbed up and up that high hill. They pushed at the rock and they pulled at the rock. Suddenly it came loose.

"Hurrah!" the people shouted. "Now all we have to do is get it down the hill."

How could they do that? Should they push the rock or pull it?

"We'd better just drag it down," they decided.

The rock was heavy and the hill was steep. Groaning and gasping, the people of Chelm managed to drag the rock almost halfway down the hill before they had to stop for a rest. As they stood around and panted, a stranger came riding by at the bottom of the hill. He heard all the weary sighs and looked up.

"What are you people trying to do?" he asked.

"Someday this rock might fall on our village," Yussel called back, "so we're trying to drag it down the hill instead."

The stranger started to laugh. "Why are you bothering to *drag* the rock?" he asked. "The hill is steep enough. Just give the rock a good push the way you want it to go, and it will roll down all by itself!"

The wise men of Chelm scratched their heads in thought.

"What a clever fellow that stranger is," they decided. "We shall make the rock roll down the hill all by itself!"

So they dragged the rock wearily all the way back up the hill and gave it a push. And, sure enough, it did roll all the way down by itself.

Sun and Moon

Once the moon was safely up and the rock was safely down, the people of Chelm began to wonder about nature. Up in the sky, they knew, was the sun as well as the moon.

"But which," they puzzled, "is more important? Is it the sun or is it the moon?"

Well, people began to argue about it, sun or moon, moon or sun. In fact, things got so bad in Chelm that people were actually shouting at each other.

"The sun is more important!"

"The moon is more important!"

"The sun!"

"The moon!"

This couldn't go on, they decided. If it did, pretty soon people were going to start hitting each other, and that would be a terrible thing to have happen in a friendly town like Chelm. So off they all went to the rabbi of Chelm and asked him, "Which is more important, the sun or the moon?"

The rabbi was a true citizen of Chelm. He thought and thought about this question for a time, then thought about it some more. At last he called the people of Chelm back to him and said, "I have the answer. The moon is more important. You see, as we all know, it shines in the night, when things would otherwise be dark. The sun, however, isn't so useful. After all, it shines during the day, when things are already light!"

The Sundial

One day, not long after settling the problem of the sun and the moon and which was more important, the wise men of Chelm made a discovery.

"Maybe the sun isn't as important as the moon. But we can still use it to tell time!"

So they had Chaim the carpenter build them a sundial.

Oh, what a beautiful sundial that was, so beautiful that people used to stop to see what time it was even when they didn't really need to know.

But the sky can't always be sunny. One day a storm came along. Rain poured down on the sundial.

"Oh, no," the people cried, "the sundial is getting wet. We can't let our beautiful sundial get wet!"

The wise men of Chelm held a meeting. They talked about the problem of the sundial getting wet, and they thought about it for long hours. At last they reached a decision.

What did the people of Chelm do? Why, they hired Chaim the carpenter to build a roof over their sundial, of course!

Hot Air

Now that the people of Chelm knew about the sun and the moon, they began to wonder about other things.

"What about winter and summer?" they said. "Everyone knows that winter is cold and summer is hot—but why it is so?"

The wise men of Chelm puzzled about this and puzzled about this. At last they went to the rabbi and asked him, "Why is winter cold and summer hot?"

"Ah, my friends, the answer is simple!" the rabbi cried. "In winter we all use our stoves day and night. Is that not so?"

The people nodded. "We do, indeed."

"Well, then! The hot air from the stoves warms up the air outside. By the time it's summer, the air has become so hot there's no need for us to keep using our stoves. So we stop. Is that not so?"

The people nodded. "It's too hot in summer to use stoves."

"Well, then! Without the stoves burning away, the air has a chance to cool off. It cools down all the way through autumn. And by the time it's winter, why the air is freezing again! So we start using our stoves once more." The rabbi folded his arms in satisfaction. "And that," he said, "is why winters are cold and summers are hot."

Fire!

One dark, moonless night early in spring, when all the people of Chelm were still using their stoves day and night to warm up the air, somebody put a little too much wood in a stove.

The wood burned. Oy, did it burn! It burned so fiercely that pretty soon the whole house was burning.

All the people of Chelm came running. "How should we put out this fire?" they cried.

"First we could draw a magic circle around it," the rabbi mused. "Then we could try holy words … "

"But rabbi!" the people cried. "What about water?"

"Water's a good idea, too."

So the people of Chelm brought bucket after bucket of water and tossed them on the burning house. At last the fire was out.

Everyone sat down to rest. They all started to wail over their misfortune, when all at once the rabbi cried, "Why, this fire was a miracle from heaven!"

"How could that be?" everyone asked.

"Well, the night is very dark, isn't it?"

"It is," they all agreed.

The rabbi smiled. "There you are! If the fire hadn't been burning so very brightly on such a dark night—why, how could we ever have seen how to put it out?"

"Why, that's right!" the people of Chelm cried. "How very fortunate we are!"

A Thief in Chelm

One night in Chelm, a night when the moon wasn't shining, a terrible thing happened. A thief broke into the synagogue, just as thieves did in big cities like Cracow and Moscow, and stole the poor box. The wise men of Chelm gathered the next morning.

"Such a scandal must never happen again," they decided.

But what could they do about it?

"I know!" Hershel the miller said. "We shall install a new poor box."

"But what's to stop that thief from simply stealing this one, too?" Yussel the baker asked.

They all thought for a long, long time.

"I know!" Hershel said again. "We shall install a new poor box, but this one we shall hang from the ceiling, right up there near the roof. Then no thief will be able to reach it."

Everyone thought this was a fine idea, a wonderful idea.

"Wait!" cried a voice from the back of the room. "If the poor box is hanging up near the roof of the synagogue, how is anyone who wants to give money going to reach it?"

Now that was a question worth thinking about. And think, the wise men of Chelm did. Cries of, "What if?" and "Yes, but ... " echoed back and forth.

And at last the wise men of Chelm came up with the answer.

"We will hang the poor box from the ceiling," they said, "up near the roof. But we shall also build a ladder so that people can reach it!"

Digging a Pit

One day, not long after the problem with the poor box, the wise men of Chelm decided that their synagogue was just too small and too old.

"We must build a new synagogue," they said.

Now, all buildings, even holy ones, need foundations if they are to stand without falling. Even the wise men of Chelm knew that! So they all picked up their shovels and set to work digging a good, deep foundation for the new synagogue.

"Wait a minute," Hershel the miller said. "What are we going to do with all the dirt we're digging up?"

Here was a problem indeed! Everyone stopped digging to stand and think. They thought and thought.

"I know!" cried Yussel the baker at last. "All we have to do is dig a new pit. And into that pit we'll dump all the dirt from this one."

Everyone was happy with that answer. They started to dig again, but then Chaim the carpenter stopped.

"Wait a minute," he said. "What will we do with all the dirt from *that* pit?"

Here was an even bigger problem. Everyone stopped digging again. They stood thinking and thinking and thinking.

"I have the answer!" Hershel cried. "We'll dig *another* pit! This one will be twice as big and twice as deep as the first pit, and into it we will shovel all the dirt from the first two pits."

"Yes!" everyone shouted. "That's it! Of course!"

And they all went back to digging.

The Chief Sage of Chelm

One day, the wise men of Chelm gathered to ask themselves the following question: "How can we make Chelm a more important place in the eyes of the world?"

"We must do something special," Hershel the miller decided.

"No, no, we must show how special we are," Chaim the carpenter argued.

"I know!" Yussel the baker cried. "We shall show the world just how wise we are, and to do that, we must name the wisest man in town the chief sage."

Everyone thought that was a wonderful idea. They thought and thought about it, and finally decided that Moishe the tailor was to be the chief sage of Chelm. Why Moishe? Why not?

"But how is everyone going to know I'm the chief sage?" Moishe asked. "There must be something special about me. All the world must know I am an important man."

The wise men of Chelm agreed. They thought it over, and at last they knew what to do. They had a fine pair of golden shoes made for Moishe to wear.

"Now everyone will know you are the chief sage of Chelm," they said.

But alas, the streets of Chelm weren't paved. As Moishe the chief sage stepped proudly out, he landed right in a mud puddle. The mud covered up all the gold. Without those golden shoes, no one in Chelm could recognize their chief sage!

"This will never do!" Moishe said. "If no one knows who I am, I–I shall resign!"

"No, no, don't do that!" the wise men of Chelm cried. "We shall find a solution to this problem."

So they had a nice pair of leather shoes made to protect the golden ones.

But when Moishe put the leather shoes over the golden shoes, no one could see even the smallest glint of gold. Without those golden shoes, no one in Chelm could recognize their chief sage.

"Everybody's ignoring me," Moishe complained. "That's not good for a chief sage."

"Of course not," the wise men of Chelm agreed.

So they had a new pair of shoes made for their chief sage. This pair had holes cut into the sides. The golden shoes shone through the holes.

But the first time Moishe the chief sage stepped out into the street, he stepped right into another mud puddle. Mud squished into the holes in the leather shoes, covering up the gold once again. Without those golden shoes, no one in Chelm could recognize their chief sage!

"This ... this is an outrage!" Moishe exclaimed.

"Don't worry," the wise men of Chelm soothed him. "We shall solve this problem yet, we promise you."

They tried stuffing straw into the holes in the leather shoes. The straw kept out the mud very well—but now it was the straw that hid the gold! The wise men of Chelm almost wept. How could they ever solve this problem?

Yet after days of careful thought, they laughed with joy. They had the answer!

"Moishe, you shall wear ordinary leather shoes on your feet," they told him, "but so that everyone shall know you are the chief sage of Chelm, you shall also wear the golden shoes. You shall wear them on your hands!"

"What a brilliant solution!" Moishe cried.

So from then on, he wore the golden shoes on his hands whenever he went out. Now everyone in Chelm could recognize their chief sage!

The Worrier of Chelm

Now that they had a chief sage to show how important they were, the people of Chelm should have been happy.

They weren't. They still spent a lot of time worrying about other things. They worried about what would happen if the sun decided to fall out of the sky. They worried about what would happen if water decided to run uphill. Indeed, the people of Chelm spent so much time worrying, they began to worry they wouldn't have any time left to do anything else!

So the wise men of Chelm met to ponder the problem. They studied it from this side and that. They talked about it and they thought about it. And at the end of all this, they came up with a solution.

"We will create a new post," they said. "From now on, we shall have an official worrier in Chelm. We will name Yussel the baker to the position, and pay him a nice weekly salary. In exchange, he will do all the worrying for everyone in Chelm!"

They all thought this was a fine solution, a wonderful solution. But just before the wise men of Chelm were to vote on the subject, one timid voice called out from the back of the room, "But if you're going to pay Yussel the baker a nice weekly salary, what has he got to worry about?"

The Cat and the Butter

Moishe the chief sage had a cat. And oy, was that cat a pest! If there was any trouble to be gotten into, you can be sure that cat was in the middle of it.

One day, Moishe's wife Zaide brought home a pound of butter. She put it on the kitchen table, meaning to put it away in a moment, and left the room. Zoom! Faster than thought, the cat was on the table, and the butter was inside the cat.

Zaide returned to find the table and the cat—but no butter.

"You thief!" she shrieked, and grabbed her rolling pin. "I'll ... I'll flatten you, that's what I'll do!"

Moishe came home to find Zaide chasing the cat around and around the kitchen. "Wait, stop!" he cried, and caught his wife by the arm. "What are you doing?"

"I'm trying to flatten that thieving cat!" she cried. "He's eaten a whole pound of butter."

"Hmmm," murmured Moishe. "Did you actually see the cat eat the butter?"

"No, but ... the cat is there and the butter is gone!"

"Hmmm," Moishe repeated. "We must test this." He put the kitchen scales on the table, and the cat on the scales.

"Look at that!" Zaide cried. "Exactly one pound! There's the butter, all right!"

"Yes," said Moishe. "But if there's the butter, then *where is the cat?*"

Neither Moishe nor Zaide could answer that.

Tea With Sugar

Now that Moishe was chief sage of Chelm, he began to realize just what a clever fellow he was. He started telling the wise men of Chelm all the wisdom he had been storing up in his brain.

"Here is a problem," Moishe said one day. "What is it that makes tea sweet?"

"Why, it's the sugar," Yussel the baker said.

"Then why do we need the teaspoon?" Moishe asked.

"To stir … "

"No, no! I'll tell you why we need the teaspoon. It is the teaspoon that sweetens the tea! After all, when you put sugar into the tea, the tea doesn't get sweet right away. It only gets sweet after you've stirred it!"

Yussel scratched his head. "But … but if it's the teaspoon that makes the tea sweet, why do we need any sugar at all?"

"Aha! Only the chief sage of Chelm would know the answer to that! It is the teaspoon that sweetens the tea, but we need the sugar as well. By watching that sugar carefully, we can see it dissolve. If it wasn't for that sign, how would we ever know when to stop stirring?"

156 Rachel the Clever

The Herring

Not only was Moishe, chief sage of Chelm, a wise man, he was also a witty one. He began to think up all sorts of puzzles and riddles to confuse his friends.

One fine summer day, while everyone was sitting outside, admiring their fine sundial under its protective roof, Moishe exclaimed, "I have a new riddle!"

"Let us hear it," Hershel the miller said.

"All right. What's purple, hangs on the wall, and whistles?"

There was a long, long silence. Then Hershel sighed. "I give up. We all give up. What's purple, hangs on the wall, and whistles?"

"A herring!" Moishe cried.

"But a herring isn't purple!"

"It is if you paint it," Moishe said.

"But a herring doesn't hang on the wall!"

"It does if you hang it there," Moishe said.

Hershel scratched his head. "But a herring doesn't whistle!"

Moishe shrugged. "Oh, I just threw that in to make the riddle tougher," he said.

A Sampling of Riddles

1993 Jeanne Seagle

Q: What do you have that can fill a room yet never
      touch anything?
A: Your voice.

Q: Who can speak in every language?
A: Echo.

Q: He spreads a net, but isn't a fisherman, and what
      he catches isn't a fish.
      What is he, and what does he catch?
A: A spider and a fly.

Q: Everybody loves me yet no one can look at me.
      What am I?
A: The sun.

Q: It's not a shirt, yet it's sewed.
      It's not a tree, yet it's full of leaves.
      It's not alive, yet it talks wisely.
      What is it?
A: A book.

Q: What living creatures weren't in Noah's ark?
A: Fish.

Q: What kind of water can you carry in a sieve?
A: Frozen water—ice.

Q: How many sides does a bagel have?
A: Two: one inside, one outside!

Q: What causes no pain, no sorrow, yet makes
       everybody weep?
A: An onion.

Q: Why does a dog wag his tail?
A: Because it would be silly for the tail to wag the
       dog!

Q: What do you have that everyone else uses more
       than you?
A: Your name.

Q: It has twelve branches.
       On every branch are four twigs.
       On every twig are seven leaves.
       What is it?
A: The year.

Q: What must every good Jew do before he drinks
       tea?
A: He must open his mouth!

Q: A man dreams that he's on a ship at sea with his
       father and mother. In the middle of the
       ocean, the ship begins to sink. Neither his
       father nor mother can swim, but he can save
       himself and only one other. It can be either
       his father or his mother. What should he do?
A: He should wake up!

Notes

Magical Tales

THE SORCERER'S APPRENTICE

Here is an example of a tale that is told in almost every country around the world in nearly identical ways. Sometimes the hero is apprenticed to a human sorcerer, sometimes to a devil, but in each case he outwits the villain and wins his freedom and the hand of his beloved through a shape-shifting contest. The oldest versions of this type of story—at least as far as we know—come from India and are at least three thousand years old.

THE DANCING DEMONS

Different versions of this folktale can be found across Europe and Asia as far west as Ireland and as far east as Japan. Each tale features some type of dancing or singing nonhuman folk, depending on each nation's folklore. In Ireland and Wales, for instance, the demons are replaced by fairies; some retellings even include the music the fairies were supposed to be singing! Demons in Jewish folklore aren't always evil beings. In a good many tales, they seem instead more like mischievous nature spirits.

CINDERELLA

"Cinderella" is almost certainly the most popular fairy tale in the world. More than nine hundred versions have been collected by folklorists from almost every country! It's also a very old fairy tale; the earliest examples we have come from Egypt and China, and are about two thousand years old. What makes this version specifically Jewish, of course, is that instead of a prince, there's a rabbi's son, while the fairy godmother is replaced by the Prophet Elijah.

THE SULTAN'S HORNS

Although this particular story comes from Morocco, it has close kin in tales from countries as far apart as Great Britain, Greece, and Afghanistan. King Midas, the same king who had that trouble with everything he touched turning to gold, is said in one version to have donkey ears, and King Mark of Cornwall, who turns up in some of the stories of King Arthur, had horse ears. One feature common to all the tales is that talking reeds give the royal secret away.

THE SON WHO WAS A SNAKE

This is a "Beauty and the Beast" story, in which the hero is trapped in a frightening animal shape because of a spell, which can only be broken when a young woman falls in love with him. What type of beast the hero becomes depends on the land in which the story is told. In Scandinavian versions, the enchanted prince is often a bear, sometimes even a polar bear, while the Brothers Grimm collected a German tale in which the hero is born looking like a hedgehog!

THE DEMON'S MIDWIFE

This tale turns up in similar forms all over the Near East and central Asia, but it's also well-known in Great Britain and Europe, although there the demons are replaced by the fairy folk. Almost all the stories carry the same kind of warning: a visitor to a magical realm mustn't eat the food there or try to take away any magical treasure, or he or she will be trapped in the other world forever. This idea may come from the Greek myth of Persephone, who was carried down to the under-world by its ruler. Because she ate six pomegranate seeds while there, she had to spend six months of every year in the underworld.

THE TRICKY SHEEP

The idea of a mischievous, shape-shifting creature who loves to play tricks on unsuspecting humans is common to a great many cultures around the world. In England, for in-stance, the Hedley Kow is the name of a tricky being very similar in the pranks he pulls to the "sheep" in this tale.

Clever Folks

RACHEL THE CLEVER

This type of story about a clever, loving wife and her riddle-solving abilities is popular throughout eastern Europe and the Near East. Only the individual riddles vary from story to story; the punchline, in which the wife proves how truly she loves her husband, remains the same. Riddle contests are found in almost every culture, and have even been used by such writers as J.R.R. Tolkien, who included a riddle contest in his fantasy novel, *The Hobbit*.

CHOOSING LOTS

There are many versions, both Jewish and non-Jewish, of this story. Sometimes it's both pieces of paper that have been marked "guilty." In other cultures, where reading isn't a common ability, the pieces of paper are replaced by pebbles, both of which have been painted black for "guilty." And in some versions, the gambler really is guilty, but escapes by his cleverness!

THE SLAVE WHO WAS A DETECTIVE

Anyone who has read Arthur Conan Doyle's stories of Sherlock Holmes will certainly appreciate this slave-hero's powers of deduction. Tales of similar deductive detectives have been told throughout the Near East and central Asia.

THE SILENT DUEL

This type of tongue-in-cheek version of the riddle contest, in which each contestant thinks the other one meant something else entirely, is popular in the New World as well as the Near East.

ONE SHOT TOO MANY

Although this tale, with its attempt at armed robbery and its clever hero, sounds as though it might have come from the newspapers of any modern city, it actually was first recorded by a folklorist in eastern Europe in the early part of this century.

THE QUESTIONS OF THE KING

Here is yet another riddle contest, but one with a catch: the riddles have no genuine answer. It's the cleverness of the riddler against that of the would-be answerer that counts. A common element of folktales around the world is that of seeing the small and seemingly helpless get the better of the rich and powerful through the use of their wits.

THE HIDDEN GOLD

This is another detection tale, this time meant as a religious fable to show that even as a child, long before he knew he was to be king of Israel, David was both wise and kind of heart.

DOING UNTO OTHERS

The idea of faking stupidity to outwit enemies turns up in many a folktale. Maybe the best-known example is in the German story of "Hansel and Gretel," in which Gretel saves herself and her brother from the wicked witch by pretending she doesn't know how to look into an oven.

THE MASTER THIEF

This is a very popular type of folktale indeed. Similar versions of it can be found around the world, particularly in Europe and Asia, and in the *History* of the Greek historian, Herodotus. Most of these tales feature some sort of graduation test or competition, in which the young thief has to perform a seemingly impossible task.

Tales of Ghosts and Other Strange Things

THE THANKFUL GHOST

Tales of grateful ghosts returning to help those who gave them an honorable burial turn up all over Europe, and are usually classed under the heading of The Grateful Dead. The rock band known as The Grateful Dead probably got their name from this!

THE GHOSTLY CONGREGATION

This spooky little story dates back to the twelfth or thirteenth century. The idea that someone about to die might be seen in a vision as already dead turns up in many folktales, though usually the vision is seen by a relative or a lover.

THE INSULTED GHOSTS

Stories of humans overhearing supernatural beings and gaining rewards from what they hear are common throughout the world. But the idea of two girl ghosts being indignant over the invasion of their privacy is uniquely Jewish!

THE RESTLESS GHOST

This is a Polish legend that dates back to the seventeenth century, but there are a good many other ghost stories about restless spirits who haunt those who broke promises made when they were still alive.

THE GILGUL

Though every culture has its tales of possession by demons, the gilgul isn't a demon at all, only a misplaced soul, or someone who has left something undone in his or her life. Once the gilgul's demands are met, it's usually quite willing to leave.

THE POET AND HIS SERVANT

There really was a Solomon ibn Gabirol, who really did live in the Spanish city of Valencia, but there's no evidence at all that he actually managed to create a robot-maid to do his cleaning! During the Middle Ages, many a scholar was accused of dabbling in magic.

THE GOLEM OF PRAGUE

This is one of the most famous Jewish "magical robot" stories. Although the golem was created to protect the Jews of Prague, some versions add a hint of danger, warning that great power can sometimes go out of control and turn on its users. It's fun to see that the same story of "The Sorcerer's Apprentice" and the water-bringing broom that nearly floods the sorcerer's home turns up here, when the golem nearly floods the rabbi's house because no one tells it to stop bringing water. Folk themes like this travel from country to country and often get attached to different stories by mistake or simply because a storyteller liked them.

Doing the Right Thing

A GOOD DEED REPAID

A very important part of Judaism is the giving of charity. There are many Jewish folktales, such as this one, which show how kindness to the needy is repaid by the saving of the kind person's life.

ONE GOLD COIN

There are two good men in this story, the poor man who follows the teachings of his religion, and the merchant who keeps his promise. In folklore, the idea of someone becoming rich because his cat is a good catcher of mice or rats is a popular one. The most well known of these stories is probably the English tale of "Dick Whittington and His Cat." Whittington was a real mayor of London who lived in the fourteenth century, but there's no proof it was his cat who helped him to that job!

THE TWO BEGGARS

A common theme in Jewish folklore is the belief that all goodness, no matter how it's disguised, can only come from God.

THROWING STONES

Although this is a Jewish fable, the moral behind it should be very familiar to Christians as well: "Do unto others as you would have them do unto you."

WHICH WAS THE TRULY PIOUS?

This is an example of what folklorists call *jokelore*, the folklore of funny stories. At the same time that it makes fun of the pompous and proud, it also points out that the true meaning of charity doesn't depend on anything but a good heart.

THE TRAPPER TRAPPED

This story of unavoidable destiny is one of a whole family of similar tales found throughout Europe and Asia. The usual form of the tale features a king who refuses to let a poor boy marry his daughter, only to be tricked by destiny into allowing that marriage. The difference here is that the merchant, who takes the place of a king in this story, gets so carried away with his hunger for revenge that he is caught in his own trap.

FAITH
This is a very old folktale, dating at least to the sixth century Indian collection of stories, the *Pantschatantra*. Similar versions have been found in the Near East and around the Mediterranean.

CAKE
Stories about dreams that warn the dreamer to mend his bad behavior can be found all over the world. One even turns up in the song, "Sit Down, You're Rockin' the Boat," from the 1950 musical, *Guys and Dolls!*

THE GOOD NEIGHBOR
This tale makes an important point: a Jew and a Christian, despite their differences, can still be good and honest friends.

The Wise Men of Chelm

ABOUT THE WISE MEN OF CHELM
Chelm was a perfectly real town in Poland. How did all these silly stories get attached to it? No one knows!
Folktales about silly people are familiar to everyone. German children were told about the fools who wept over an ax that might someday fall and hit someone who hadn't even been born yet. English children heard the story of the six sillies who are sure one of them is missing, because the silly doing the counting keeps forgetting to count himself. Aesop told a fable for Greek children about a silly, greedy dog who lost his bone in a pond because he thought its reflection was a second bone and he tried to eat them both. And in Africa, Bantu children know about a foolish lion who is scared away by the booming echo of a tiny bush rat's voice.
Chelm isn't the only town of silly people to be found in the world of folklore. The wise men of Chelm are surely brothers to the wise men of Gotham—an equally real town in England—who are supposed to have tried to do things like

trapping a cuckoo behind walls, only to have the bird fly away because no one thought to include a roof in their trap!

A Sampling of Riddles

Riddle and logic puzzles are found in every country and throughout history. Some of the riddles in this chapter, such as those about echoes or the sun, are known in one form or another to almost everyone, but others are specially Jewish. The Jews have always had a love of learning, so many of their riddles involve books or religious lessons, such as the riddle about Noah's ark. A bagel, for anyone who has never tasted one, is a type of Jewish roll shaped like a doughnut. Bagels are traditionally cut in half and served either buttered or filled with cream cheese and lox, which is a form of smoked salmon.